"You ...
you...

Melissa's eyes flew open and she stiffened, her pulse speeding up dramatically as she realized that Sean Culhane was standing by the sunken tub. He was clad only in his jeans.

Melissa had seldom felt more vulnerable. "Sean!" she exclaimed. Bringing her arms up, she crossed them protectively in front of her. At least the roiling water offered some shield against his scrutiny.

With almost ritual deliberation his hands slid up her arms and over her smooth, naked shoulders before gently encircling the slim column of her throat. His thumbs stroked lightly at the hollow above the joining of her collarbone.

Her water-warmed skin was very sensitive. The barest brush of contact sent a quiver through her, racing along the network of nerve endings.

Melissa's huge gray eyes had gone smoky with emotion. "You promised—" she whispered. "You said nothing would happen."

"I said nothing would happen that you didn't want to happen," he corrected her softly . . .

Dear Reader:

By now our new cover treatment—with larger art work—is familiar to you. But don't forget that, in a sense, our new cover reflects what's been happening *inside* SECOND CHANCE AT LOVE books. We're constantly striving to bring you fresh and original romances with unexpected twists and delightful surprises. We introduce promising new writers on a regular basis. And we aim for variety by publishing some romances that are funny, some that are poignant, some that are "traditional," and some that take an entirely new approach. SECOND CHANCE AT LOVE is constantly evolving to meet your need for "something new" in your romance reading.

At the same time, we *haven't* changed the successful editorial concept behind each SECOND CHANCE AT LOVE romance. We work hard to make sure every romance we publish is a satisfying read. And at SECOND CHANCE AT LOVE we've consistently maintained a reputation for being a line of the highest quality.

So, just like the new covers, SECOND CHANCE AT LOVE romances are satisfyingly familiar—yet excitingly different—and better than ever.

Happy reading,

Ellen Edwards

Ellen Edwards, Senior Editor
SECOND CHANCE AT LOVE
The Berkley Publishing Group
200 Madison Avenue
New York, N.Y. 10016

P.S. Do you receive our SECOND CHANCE AT LOVE and TO HAVE AND TO HOLD newsletter? If not, be sure to fill out the coupon in the back of this book, and we'll send you the newsletter free of charge four times a year.

ENCORE

CAROLE BUCK

**SECOND CHANCE AT LOVE
BOOK**

ENCORE

Second Chance at Love books are published by
The Berkley Publishing Group
200 Madison Avenue, New York, NY 10016

ENCORE

CHAPTER ONE

MELISSA STEWART UNDRESSED with the unthinking grace of a professional dancer, draping her clothes neatly over the straight-back metal chair by the examination table. She didn't like this cold pastel-toned room, with its sterile high-tech trappings. She didn't want to be here. Only the pain in her right knee—now mercifully, if temporarily, dulled from lancing agony to a throbbing ache—kept her from running out of the clinic and never coming back.

Run out of the clinic? Melissa's brow pleated as she considered this unlikely possibility. Grimacing, she stripped off her black linen slacks, baring marble-smooth thighs and long sleek legs. She'd been lucky she'd been able to walk *into* it!

She'd taken off everything but her peach nylon and lace camisole top and panties before she sensed that there was someone else in the room with her. Stiffening like

1

a wild creature, she whirled, every nerve ending in her slender body clamoring in instinctive alarm. Her long raven-black fall of hair fanned out silkily as she turned.

It couldn't be!

Her crystal-gray eyes widened with shock. The blood drained slowly from her oval face, leaving her delicately molded features alabaster pale.

"Sean!" The name came out in a strangled whisper. Whether it was an invocation of a cherished memory— or a protest against a ghost from the past—it was impossible to tell.

"I always liked you in pink, Melissa," the intruder said in a conversational tone. He was lounging casually against the doorjamb of what she assumed must be the bathroom. His hands rested on his trim hips; his manner was nonchalant and utterly relaxed.

Melissa was not fooled by his air of apparent indolence. The superbly conditioned body sheathed in the civilized accoutrements of an elegantly tailored navy business suit was capable of attacking with lightning speed and bruising power. This man hadn't been nicknamed "The Lion" simply because of his mane of thick tawny hair and disconcerting green-gold eyes. Like the king of the jungle, he was a creature of deceptively lazy grace at times. He was also supremely dangerous when aroused.

"This color happens to be peach," she corrected him pointedly, fighting to gain her equilibrium. "And what are you doing here?"

Melissa's head was spinning. *You've danced before heaven knows how many thousands of people in nothing more than skin-tight leotards and tights,* she told herself, over the beat of her hammering heart. *And you never blinked an eye at that! You are not going to turn into some quiveringly modest idiot because your one and only former lover happens to catch you in your underwear!* How was it possible that Sean Culhane was standing right here before her in her clinic examination room? What weird twist of fate...

"Peach—pink, close enough. I always liked you *out* of pink, too." He smiled, choosing to deal with her first comment only. It was a slow, teasing grin, revealing strong white teeth that contrasted attractively with his tanned skin. A roguish dimple creased one corner of his sensual male mouth. It was a disarming, deliberately seductive expression. Despite herself, Melissa felt a compelling stir of attraction.

She took a deep, controlling breath. "I really don't care what you 'always liked,' Sean Culhane," she said flatly, drawing herself up in a single, supple motion. He wasn't going to get to her. Not after all this time!

But, Lord, he was still a magnificent, emphatically masculine animal—tall, proud, and confident to the point of arrogance. She had forgotten, or had forced herself to deny, his natural, sexual charisma and the effect it had on her.

"There was a time you did care," he replied quietly, pushing away from the door. He deftly reknotted his discreetly patterned wine silk tie. She caught the flash of a heavy gold ring on his right hand as he did so. It was the coveted ring of a Super Bowl champion, she knew. She wondered fleetingly if it was the one he'd had when they'd first met, or the one he'd won after they'd broken up. "There was a time when you cared very much."

"That was long ago," she told him steadily, daintily moistening her upper lip with the tip of her tongue. She saw a molten gleam of something disturbingly primitive stir in the depths of his eyes. His jungle-cat gaze swept down her hungrily. The look made her want to cover herself up and melt into his arms—both at the same time. Involuntarily, in a motion as graceful as any she had ever used onstage, she started to bring her hands up in an ancient gesture of feminine modesty. Realizing what she was doing—and how much it betrayed—she controlled the movement, but not before Sean recognized it for what it was.

The curving of his lips told her he was aware of the reaction he was provoking. "I don't call five years a long time, Melissa."

"I call it a lifetime," she returned, tilting her chin with reckless spirit. "I've changed."

"Have you?" he challenged, a certain harshness coming into his smooth voice. "How much, I wonder?"

He closed the distance between them in three lithe strides, taking her as a natural predator takes its prey.

As a principal dancer for the Manhattan Ballet Theater, Melissa had been made love to by any number of different men—onstage. She was accustomed to the hot press of skin on skin, to the intimacy of physical contact. But there was a world of difference, a world of pulsating, soaring sensation, between the pretense of the pas de deux and the passionate reality of finding herself in Sean's arms once again.

Her nostrils flared at the clean, distinctly masculine smell of his skin and the faintly spicy fragrance of his cologne. It was evocatively familiar, awakening a host of memories inside her. She was dizzyingly conscious of the feel of her small breasts straining against the delicate fabric of her camisole as he pulled her firmly against the unyielding wall of his chest. She was acutely aware of how one of his large, strong-fingered hands slipped caressingly down her spine and curved possessively over her firm bottom, molding her to him, teaching her once again the achingly sweet perfection of their bodies' fit.

His other hand came up to cup the back of her head, his fingers tangling in her night-dark tumble of hair. He turned her face up to his, exerting his control over her gently but unmistakably.

Melissa's heart was pounding the way it did at the

end of a demanding solo when she stood, trembling in the spotlight, listening to the applause as it welled up out of the audience and embraced her. She felt a hot flush of excitement surge through her, filling her bloodstream with liquid fire and turning her bones to jelly.

She didn't fight Sean. How could she? She was too busy fighting herself. All the feelings she had tried to lock away or to channel into her dancing during the past five years were suddenly on the loose again.

"Sean—"

His mouth came down, unerringly, on her slightly parted lips, drinking in their sweetness. After a few moments he deepened the kiss, his tongue moving with teasing skill at first, then with increasing demand.

Melissa made a soft sound deep in her throat. She couldn't—*wouldn't*—allow this to happen to her again! Yet even as her mind protested, her body was welcoming Sean's touch.

Muscle memory, dancers called it. It was what allowed them to store thousands of complicated dance steps and combinations within their bodies until the right musical or mental cue triggered their release into the smooth flow of choreography. Melissa had never considered the possibility that her highly trained body would have retained the instantly responsive memory of Sean's lovemaking as well.

Then, suddenly, it was over. Sean held her away from him abruptly and took a step back. There was a pagan cast to the glittering in his gem-toned eyes as he studied her from beneath half-lowered lids. She felt his gaze rove over her assessingly, marking the soft surrender of her faintly reddened lips and the provocative thrust of her small but exquisitely formed breasts against her camisole.

"You haven't changed that much, Melissa," he drawled slowly, one tawny brow quirking upward. "You still smell like a flower garden after a spring rain and the taste of you is still enough to make a man drunk." His mouth curved into a brief, hard smile. "And, God knows, you still feel the same."

Melissa caught her breath, angry color staining her high cheekbones. "That wasn't what I was talking—"

The door to the examination room swung open at this point, admitting a shambling bear of a middle-aged man in a slightly wrinkled white lab coat.

"Sorry to keep you waiting, Melissa," he said absently. "I'm afraid I've been running behind schedule ever since—Sean! Frank Burke mentioned you'd been in about your shoulder. Is that . . . but what are you doing in here?"

"It's just a minor mix-up," Sean explained genially. "The nurse must have thought I'd finished with the room when she sent Melissa in. No harm done."

Melissa shot him an indignant glare. *No harm done?!*

"Oh, I see," Dr. Goldberg nodded, apparently oblivious to the charged atmosphere in the room. He glanced back and forth between Melissa and Sean a bit curiously. It was impossible to tell if he found anything peculiar in the fact that while Sean was fully dressed, Melissa was clad only in her lingerie. "Ah, do you two know each other?" he asked finally.

"We've met," Melissa jumped in, determined to take the initiative.

"We're old friends," Sean amended with infuriating calm. "In fact, I'm the one who recommended she come to this clinic in the first place."

"Really?" The medical man seemed interested.

"It was about five years ago," Sean affirmed. "Aren't you cold, Melissa?"

"I—what?" The question was so totally unexpected, and the tone of voice so obviously baiting, that Melissa was left momentarily wordless. The *nerve* of him!

"I seem to remember dancers feel comfortable only when they're wrapped up in about a dozen layers of clothing. You must be freezing wearing just that—" He gestured solicitously, but his eyes were mocking. "You're trembling," he added.

She was. But it had nothing to do with the chill and everything to do with him. Melissa had to bite her tongue to keep from informing him of that.

"Thank you for your concern." Though her words were sweetly civil, the look on her face informed him eloquently of what he could do with his concern. With a poise she was far from feeling she moved over to the examination table and picked up the functional white robe that had been laid out for her. With what she hoped was an air of blithe indifference, she slipped it on and turned to Dr. Goldberg. "I'm ready when you are," she said. "If, of course, you're quite finished in here, Sean?"

"I'm finished with the room," he answered blandly. There was a faintly provocative emphasis on the last word. "Sorry if I disturbed you, Melissa."

"Oh, don't worry. You didn't," she replied, matching his tone. His eyes narrowed as she felt a small surge of satisfaction. She couldn't disguise the fact that she had responded to him physically a few minutes before, but she *could* convincingly act as though that response had meant nothing to her. Melissa met his gaze unblinkingly.

"I'll be seeing you," Sean said after a moment. While his nod of leave-taking included both Melissa and Dr. Goldberg, she had the distinct impression his final words were a message of promise—and warning—for her alone.

The examination was thorough, time-consuming, and occasionally uncomfortable, but Melissa endured it without complaint. She knew that for all his rumpled appearance and apparent absentmindedness, David Goldberg was a superb and caring doctor. She also recognized that this time she was confronted with a physical problem that couldn't be treated with the time-honored dancer's combination of home remedies and stoic acceptance.

"You can get dressed, Melissa," Dr. Goldberg instructed her at last. "I'll talk to you in my office."

Melissa slid off the examination table in a feather-light movement, controlling a wince as her foot touched the floor. "Am I going to be able to play the violin again?" she asked in a gallant attempt at humor.

"In my office," he repeated firmly.

Melissa's posture was faultlessly erect, and her features became serious when she took a seat opposite the doctor's booklittered and paper-strewn desk a few minutes later. Only a faint line of anxiety between her thin dark brows, and the clenching and unclenching of her hands revealed her tension.

I wish I smoked, she thought suddenly. *At least it would give me something to do until the ax falls.*

The doctor got right down to business. After quickly reviewing Melissa's case, he delivered his verdict.

"I'm not recommending surgery right now, although it's definitely in the cards if you don't stop demanding the impossible of your body," he said. "You've been dancing since you were what, five or six? The strain is starting to tell. You've got to let up, Melissa. You're going to have to stay off that knee for two months."

"Two months!" Two months without dancing was an eternity. Two months without dancing would mean weeks of additional practice to get back to performance-level condition. The prospect appalled her.

"Total rest for the first month," he elaborated. "I'll prescribe a program of physical therapy for you. After four weeks, depending on how things look, you may be able to start doing some limited workouts. But I don't want you to so much as think about performing or dancing full-out until mid-November."

"I'll stay out a month."

"That's not good enough."

"Six weeks?"

He frowned. "Look, I am not going to sit here and

haggle with you. Your health is at stake. I realize you can probably force yourself to keep going despite this injury. But, if you do, I warn you, it's nothing you'll be able to carry off for very long. You have a treatable problem at this point—*if* you handle it sensibly. If you don't, I can promise you'll be a candidate for major surgery or *retirement* within six months."

There was a tense silence. Melissa bent her head, staring down at her hands. Her slender fingers were interlaced into white-knuckled knots. After a few moments her chin came up proudly. She tossed her dark hair back in a determined gesture.

"Melissa?" Dr. Goldberg probed hopefully.

She gave him a philosophic smile and a tiny shrug. "Just tell me what I have to do."

To Melissa's surprise Sean was sitting in the clinic's plant-filled outer lobby when she finished with Dr. Goldberg. It was lunchtime, and Sean was the only person there. He was waiting in a chair in one corner, engrossed in *The Wall Street Journal*. For a moment she allowed herself the luxury of just looking at him.

She'd seen countless pictures of him in the past five years. Even after his retirement as one of pro football's best-known quarterbacks three years before, he'd stayed in the news. His successful business activities and his involvement in numerous charities kept him in the public eye, and he'd gained new celebrity recently with a move into television sportscasting.

But it was different having him here, in the flesh, just a few feet away from her. Her fingers itched to tousle his stylishly cut, tawny thatch of hair. She wanted to touch the strong planes of his cheeks, to trace the fine, whitened line of the scar that ran up out of his right brow, to stroke the sensuous curve of his lips. She knew the powerful width of shoulder, the tapering leanness of torso and belly, and the taut strength of thigh and leg that his sophisticated, tailored clothing only hinted at. She wanted to feel—

Sean looked up suddenly, as though sensing her presence. Green-gold eyes met gray ones in wordless communication. He rose in a smooth athletic movement, his lips forming a warm but slightly questioning smile. Melissa felt the separation of five years and the tensions of their most recent encounter fall away.

"What—what are you doing here?" she asked, shaking off the temptation to succumb to emotion. Her tone was distinctly wary.

"Waiting for you," he replied simply. "I thought you might need a friend once Dave got through with you."

"Oh."

"Bad news?" The query was gentle.

Melissa made a small gesture of disgust and shifted her heavy canvas tote bag from one hand to the other. "It's my knee. I have to stop dancing for two months."

His brows contracted briefly. "I'm sorry," he said quietly. "I know how you must feel."

"Do you?" she countered bitterly. Sean had never understood what her dancing meant to her. That had been the crux of all their problems. "I appreciate your sympathy, Sean, but I doubt that you have any idea how I feel."

A spark of anger flared in his eyes, but was swiftly controlled. "I have a damn good idea, Melissa," he returned. "I spent most of my third season in pro ball on the bench because of a shoulder injury. I know what it's like to sit on the sidelines—or to stand in the wings— and watch somebody else doing what you'd give anything to be able to do yourself."

She bit her lip. She hadn't intended to be bitchy, but she'd needed to lash out. Sean had always been a lightning rod for her stormiest emotions.

"I'm sorry," she apologized sincerely. "That was a stupid thing to say. It's just that I'm so—so—" She shook her head, unable to come up with the right words. "It was—it was nice of you to wait for me," she finished lamely.

It had been more than nice. It had been the gesture of a sensitive man who was not afraid to act on his perceptions about other people's needs. Yet this was the same man who had hurt her so badly five years before with his lack of understanding. The same man who, barely an hour before, had taken advantage of her on a very basic physical level.

"No problem, sweetheart. You're entitled." Small lines of good humor crinkled at the corners of his eyes as he smiled at her. "To tell the truth, I did have an ulterior motive in waiting for you."

"You did?" Her suspicions returned in force, wiping out the unexpected surge of pleasure she'd felt at his offhand use of the endearment.

"Um-hm. I thought I might take you to lunch. I hate to eat alone."

"Oh, really?"

"Besides, you're a cheap date."

"A cheap date?" she repeated with a mixture of disbelief and indignation. "Don't tell me that 'Lion' Culhane has been reduced to prowling around medical clinics trying to pick up temporarily disabled women who won't cost him very much! Just what, exactly, do you mean by 'cheap date'?"

"You make it sound so sleazy," he protested with a doleful sigh.

"I suppose you'd call this your good deed for the day?"

"I was a Boy Scout once," he informed her.

"I can imagine what kind of merit badges you earned." She frowned.

Sean grinned at her appreciatively, his eyes glinting with flirtatious fun. "Okay, okay. I surrender. I'll take back the crack about the cheap date. I was referring only to your eating habits." His gaze raked her slender form in unabashed assessment. The subtle styling of her white silk shirt and the trim fit of her black linen slacks emphasized the fragility of her body. The fashionably wide multihued belt that boldly wrapped her middle underscored the narrowness of her waist.

"What's wrong with my eating habits?"

"Not a thing if you subscribe to the misguided notion that the human body can survive on an uninterrupted diet of yogurt and low-calorie soda."

She sniffed disdainfully. "You're a fine one to talk. Who was it who used to whip up that disgusting mixture of goat's milk, dessicated liver granules, and raw eggs?"

"I never ate dessicated anything in my life!"

"But you admit you *did* drink raw eggs."

"Coach's orders."

"I think you did it because it seemed like a macho way to eat eggs," she declared.

"That could well be, sweetheart. Machismo is a priority requirement for pro quarterbacks. But, now that I've hung up my cleats, I'm into eating eggs scrambled or sunny-side up. So, what do you say to lunch?"

Melissa hesitated, regretting the return to the initial issue. There was an exhilarating familiarity in trading words with Sean. Their affair five years ago had been an intensely passionate one, but it had been spiced with many humorous verbal battles.

"Please," he added, watching the various expressions flicker over her pale features. "I'd like you to have lunch with me, Melissa."

It was like standing, poised in the wings, waiting for an entrance cue. She was sharply conscious of the twin butterflies of anxiety and anticipation fluttering in the pit of her stomach. She made her decision.

"All right," she said simply.

In deference to Melissa's knee injury and presumed difficulty in walking, they chose a modest bistro just a block from the clinic. It was a pleasant restaurant, typical of the friendly, unpretentious establishments that dotted Manhattan's Upper West Side.

Melissa sensed the ripple of interest that ran through the patrons as they entered. More than a few pairs of eyes, male and female alike, followed them as the restaurant's owners led them to a table near the back. The attention was for Sean, she knew. His celebrity had bothered her when they'd first begun seeing each other; she hadn't liked the idea of having his spotlight shine on a relationship she cherished as private. She had a modest celebrity of her own now, and while she still preferred to leave the glare of the lights for the stage, she'd developed a quiet confidence in her ability to deal with the public.

She still didn't like the distinctly inviting looks Sean was getting from several of the casually but chicly dressed women diners.

Their waiter, a slim, bluejeaned young man with an engaging grin, hustled over. "The specials of the day are printed on the blackboard," he announced cheerfully, gesturing. "My name is Bryan and—oh, my God!" His eyes widened almost comically as he stared at Melissa. "Do you know who you are?" he asked excitedly. "I mean, of course you do! You're Melissa Stewart, aren't you!"

Surprised, she smiled and nodded.

"Oh, wow, I think you're just terrific! Really, you're my absolute favorite at MBT! I saw you on that dance special on public TV about a week ago. And I managed to get standing room when you did *Swan Lake* with Yuri Volnoy. I just about died. You were so beautiful."

Melissa glanced across the table at Sean, glimpsing a peculiar tightening in his features. It puzzled her. "Thank you very much, Bryan," she replied sincerely. "Are you a dancer by any chance?" He moved well. She knew that many of the young waiters and waitresses in the city were would-be performers of one kind or another.

"Yeah, but I'm between jobs right now," he told her. "I'm up for a part in the road company of a Broadway show, though. I'm your basic chorus-line gypsy."

"I hope it works out for you. Good luck."

"Thanks. Well, ah, I'll let you figure out what you want to eat."

"You have a fan," Sean commented after Bryan had walked away.

"It's still a bit strange to me," she admitted. "A few people know me now that I'm a principal with Manhattan, but there's a big difference between what I look like onstage and off." She looked at him. There was something odd about his expression. "Are you . . . irritated because he didn't recognize you?" she asked hesitantly.

Sean shook his head. "My ego isn't that fragile. A lot of people don't recognize me. To tell the truth, I like it that way. Being stared at and grabbed can get tiresome."

"I suppose that would depend upon who was doing the grabbing," she observed blandly.

He chuckled. Reaching across the table, he briefly captured one of her hands, stroking his fingers lightly down the back of it. "Ouch. Maybe you have changed, after all. I don't remember quite so many edges. It probably has something to do with becoming a star."

"I'm not a star," she demurred. "I certainly wouldn't class myself with Baryshnikov or Makarova—" His touch triggered a tremor of reaction up the length of her arm. She made a small instinctive movement of withdrawal. He released her immediately.

"True," he said mildly. "You're not Russian."

"You know what I mean, Sean."

"Still, you have been attracting a lot of good press during the past few years," he commented. "I saw the *Time* magazine spread a couple of months back. The one that was wall-to-wall pictures of you and What's-his-name Volnoy."

"Yuri." She smiled. "He's something special."

Sean's tawny brows rose. "Special professional or special personal?"

The question caught her by surprise. He sounded almost . . . what? Jealous? But that couldn't be.

"Just special special," she said quietly.

"Hmmm." It was a neutral sound.

They both retreated into a silent study of the blackboard menu. Melissa regretted the awkwardness. The truth was, despite Yuri's well-known practice of turning his dancing partners into bed partners, theirs was a strictly platonic relationship. Yet something inside her kept her from revealing this to Sean.

Bryan materialized by the table a few moments later and took their orders: a spinach salad and a Perrier with lime for Melissa, a rare steak sandwich and draft beer for Sean.

Melissa unfolded her dark-red linen napkin after the waiter moved away. "Incidentally," she began, "why were you at the clinic today? Dr. Goldberg said something about your shoulder?"

"I had a slight misunderstanding with a wall."

"I beg your pardon?"

"I was playing handball at my club and ran into a wall. It threw my shoulder out."

"How's the wall?" she inquired mischievously.

"Recovering nicely, thank you." He grinned wryly. "Tell me about your knee. Is it the same problem as before?"

"A variation on the same theme," she replied. It had been a sprained knee that had prompted her first visit to the clinic five years before. Sean had discovered her trying to nurse the injury herself, and had all but dragged her off for professional treatment. He'd dismissed her protest that the center was for sports medicine by telling her that as far as he could see she demanded more of her body than any athlete he knew. And the clinic had the best sports medical men in town.

"Too bad," he sympathized. "What happened?"

"I was dancing *Giselle* Sunday afternoon. During intermission, when I was in my dressing room stretching out and smelling my flowers—"

"Smelling your flowers? What flowers?"

Melissa smiled, her eyes sparkling. "They're something of a backstage mystery," she confided. "For the past—oh—three years, I've been getting a beautiful boquet of pink tea roses and baby's breath every time I dance. But there's never any card and no hint of who sends them."

"An unknown admirer, no doubt."

"Exactly. I've tried everything from begging to bribery to pry a name out of the florist, but nothing's worked." She looked wistful. "I wish I knew who's been sending them. They've become my good luck charm. Sometimes, before a performance, if I feel a little off, all I have to do is smell my flowers and I know somebody out there is pulling for me."

There was a brief pause as Bryan returned with their food. He served it deftly, leaving them with a jaunty wish for a good meal.

"Okay, so your knee kicked up during intermission," Sean prompted, then groaned. "Sorry, that was a lousy pun."

She laughed. "You're forgiven. It *did* start to cause problems during intermission. Poor Rex Castleberry. He was dancing the part of Albrecht. He had to do most of the work during our Act Two pas de deux."

"Why didn't you refuse to go on?"

"I couldn't! We were only halfway through the ballet. The audience was waiting. Besides," she sighed, picking up her fork and spearing a mushroom out of her salad, "there was no one at the theater to cover for me. It's barely the start of the season and a good third of the company is injured." She nibbled at the mushroom with a thoughtful expression. "We've got the same problem New York does. The first string is hurting and our bench strength is way down."

Sean came close to choking on a bite of his steak sandwich. He cleared his throat with a healthy gulp of beer. "What did you say?" he asked incredulously.

"I was talking about your former football team. With Willis and Dumbrowski out and Pearson and Nardo limping around on the sidelines, New York's defense is pretty thin." She was more than a little pleased at being able to rattle off the spiel so knowledgeably. The half-stunned, half-admiring look on Sean's face was wonderful to behold, Melissa mused.

"How the hell do you know about all that?"

Melissa took a small sip of mineral water, fighting to suppress a smile. "I may be just a dumb dancer, Sean, but I do read the sports pages every once in a while."

Of course she hadn't read them before she'd met him. Sean had made her realize how essentially unaware of the outside world she and most of her ballet cohorts were. He'd sparked something inside her. Because of him she'd begun reading, going to plays and museums, and even taking classes toward a degree at N.Y.U.

Sean frowned. "I never thought you were just a dumb anything, Melissa," he said flatly.

"Well—"

"But you didn't know anything about football when we first met."

"And you couldn't tell a tutu from a *tour jeté!*"

"Sweetheart, if you were in the tutu, I guarantee I'd know the difference."

A quiver of pleasurable excitement ran up Melissa's

spine. Sean's lightly spoken words held a disconcerting hint of passion. The darkening of his eyes to a deep jade held her mesmerized for a long moment.

Her pulse quickening, Melissa finally lowered her gaze to her plate. Taking a slow, deep breath, she summoned up a cool version of her practiced dancer's smile, not caring that it felt a little crooked. Finally she looked back up at him. Sean's leanly molded features were schooled into an enigmatic expression.

"You always did have a way of getting down to basics," Melissa said evenly, picking up her fork again.

"The jock mentality. I'm sorry if I've offended your delicate artistic sensibilities."

"You didn't," she replied after a moment. "It's just that . . . I wouldn't want you to waste your time on passes that are bound to be incomplete."

The deliberately voiced sports metaphor seemed to amuse him. "I guess I'll have to change my game plan."

They finished their meal rather quickly after that, their conversation all chitchat on the surface, all unspoken tensions below. Melissa barely restrained a sigh of relief when Sean rose after paying the bill and courteously moved to pull her chair back for her. She graciously but absently acknowledged Bryan's grinning farewell. Her mind was in a whirl. Physically she was conscious of only two things—the throbbing in her knee and the firm grip of Sean's fingers on her arm as he escorted her out of the restaurant.

They paused outside on the sidewalk, pedestrians jostling by them in the golden fall afternoon sunshine.

"Well," Melissa said, tilting her head back to look him squarely in the eyes. Her expression was cameo calm. She *had* changed in five years. "I suppose this is good-bye. Lunch was lovely, Sean. Thank you."

An errant breeze blew a long silky strand of her hair across her face. Before she could react, Sean reached forward and brushed it back into place; the faintly callused tip of one finger lingered briefly on the sensitive outer curve of her ear.

"I want to see you again, Melissa."

Her gray eyes widened, then lowered. "Why?" The single syllable held a wealth of emotion.

"Because you're something—someone—unique."

"Unique? To whom? You?" Melissa tossed her head and gave a short, humorless laugh. "Come on, Sean. I read more than the sports pages, you know. You always were as good at playing games off the field as on, and since your retirement—" She raised her brows significantly. "I've been out of the corps for five years. I have no intention of auditioning for your private chorus line."

His green eyes narrowed and she could sense the anger that rippled through him. When he spoke, his voice was carefully controlled. "As you said earlier, five years is a long time. I'm a man, not a monk. But you're still the only woman I ever asked to marry me."

CHAPTER TWO

MELISSA'S BREATH CAUGHT achingly at the top of her throat. Even had she been able to find an appropriate response in those first few seconds, she would not have been able to utter it. Why was Sean bringing this up now? Why, after so long a separation and so much silence?

"You do remember my proposing to you, Melissa?"

She swallowed, her hand tightening convulsively on the strap of her tote bag. "Yes—yes, I remember," she replied, her voice brittle. "I also remember that less than a week after you proposed you decided it wasn't going to work."

"I decided?" It came out in a hiss. A passerby brushed close to him, drawing a quick, savage stare. "It seems to me it was your mother and you who decided that!"

She paled. "My mother had nothing to do with it!"

"She had everything to do with it."

"The only thing my mother did was to warn me that you'd try to make me stop dancing. And she turned out to be right about that, didn't she, Sean?" Her dove-soft gray eyes had gone stormy with memory. "You didn't ask me to marry you. You delivered an ultimatum: you or dancing."

The strong line of his jaw clenched with temper. "If you're accusing me of not wanting to run a bad second in your life to ballet, I confess! I was guilty of that. Damn it, Melissa, I wanted you to be my *wife,* not an occasional bed partner who fit me in around matinees and guest appearances."

The pain in her knee was nothing compared with the agony that seared through her as she heard his words. She had loved Sean wildly, deliriously, five years before. He had filled her life as nothing had before, nor since. That he so badly misunderstood what she had felt for him...

She dug her nails into her palms, biting the inside of her lip to keep it from quivering. *You will not cry,* she told herself.

"If—if that's what you think of me," she got out in a low voice, "why would you want to see me again?"

"Let's just say that after five years without you I've finally decided to settle for what I can get."

"No!" She shook her head in anguished rejection.

"Yes. You're not the only one who's changed." His smile was mocking and did not reach his implacable eyes. She flinched as he reached forward and ran his thumb down the curve of her cheek. The casual but sensuous trail burned like a brand of possession. "I'll be in touch."

With that he turned and began to walk away.

"I'm not in the book!" she called after him defiantly.

He didn't break stride or glance back, but Melissa thought she saw his broad shoulders shake. He was laughing.

* * *

While Melissa did her best to put the encounter with Sean out of her mind, the memory of it clung unshakably through the rest of the day and into the next. His parting words kept ringing in her ears and this time, unlike five years before, she couldn't summon up the compelling, drugging music of the dance to drown them out.

She'd been twenty-one when she'd met Sean. Her mother had taken her to her first dance class when she was five. She'd been taking lessons daily at age ten. At twelve she'd been selected as a scholarship student at the MBT's school. Six years after that she'd been chosen to join the corps. Her elevation to soloist came three years later.

Her devotion to dancing and her mother's combination of ambition and protectiveness had sheltered her from most of life's hard realities and from its heady pleasures as well. Her existence was, in many ways, as circumscribed and as chaste as that of a novice nun.

And then Sean Culhane appeared on the scene.

At twenty-nine he was the media's darling, for his accomplishments on—and his exploits off—the football field. His background was monied, upper class, and Ivy League.

They'd met at a party given by a wealthy Manhattan businessman who was one of the MBT's most generous patrons and part owner of the pro team Sean played for. Her attraction for Sean Culhane had been instantaneous. Two weeks after being introduced they were lovers. Four months after that, for a few glorious days, they had been engaged. Then, abruptly, it was over.

Her mother, Verna, had never approved of the relationship, and even though she had offered all the right words of sympathy when the time came, Melissa had seen the gleam of satisfaction in her eyes at the end of the affair. That look had changed things between them. It created a rift that persisted until her mother's death, three years later.

Seeing Sean again brought everything flooding back. But this time she had to face the tide, not dam it up. She couldn't dance away from the hurt now.

A long list of excruciatingly mundane errands offered some distraction from the memories on Wednesday. Some distraction, but not enough. By the end of the evening she was reduced to grooming her cat, Nijinsky.

She spent a profoundly troubled night, alternating between half-waking dreams of dancing, and erotic fantasies about Sean. The aching warmth between her thighs and the yearning swell of her small breasts were far more shattering to her uncertain peace of mind than the gnawing pain in her knee.

Certain that she wasn't going to be able to endure another two days, much less two months, without doing *something*, Melissa greeted the early hours of Thursday morning with the decision to attend company class.

Located on the fifth level of the New York State Theater at Lincoln Center, the MBT rehearsal hall was like countless other rehearsal halls around the world. Rectangular. Austere. One wall was completely mirrored. The opposite one was lined with a long wooden bar that had been polished slick by the constant grip of dancers' hands. The smell of sweat and striving permeated the air.

How much of my life have I spent in places like this? Melissa wondered suddenly. *How much?*

She'd found an unobtrusive place in the corner by the door, near the piano. She sat with her long jean-clad legs spread wide. Underneath the faded denim her right knee was carefully wrapped in an Ace bandage.

The vibrations from the piano accompaniment— Tchaikovsky, pounded out in emphatic tempo—ran tauntingly through her body. Forcing herself to ignore the lure of it, Melissa leaned forward effortlessly, supporting herself on her elbows. To most people, her position would appear peculiar and even painful. To a ballet dancer, conditioned from an early age to turn out from the hip, it was a perfectly comfortable, even relaxing, posture.

"The spirit is willing but the flesh is weak, eh?"

Starting slightly, Melissa turned and looked up into the aristocratic face of Bruno Franchiese, the MBT's creative director. He was a whippet-lean man in his early sixties with dark darting eyes and an unruly shock of silver hair. Part artist, part executive, he was a martinet with the heart of a marshmallow.

Melissa smiled as he hunkered down beside her in a smooth movement. Although Franchiese had retired at the peak of his dancing career nearly three decades before, he had the athletic ease of a man in his early thirties.

"The prodigal daughter has returned," she told him.

"You could not stay away," he chuckled with an understanding nod. "Brava. You have true dedication."

"I'm suffering from true frustration at the moment," she replied candidly, a rueful look in her gray eyes. "I don't know how I'm going to make it through two months without dancing."

"Hmmm, you must he careful." A roguish glint appeared in his dark eyes. "If you will listen to the advice of an older dancer—have an affair, but don't get married."

Hot color flooded up into her cheeks. She wasn't shocked by the comment itself. Franchiese was given to dispensing personal advice to his dancers whether they asked for it or not. What did embarrass her was how she instantly conjured up a vivid mental image of herself, lying naked in Sean's arms, in response to his words.

"I don't think—there's not much likelihood of that," she said finally.

He shrugged casually. "I have been married three times. Twice I got married when I was out because of an injury. Twice I got divorced when I started to dance again. My third wife I married after I stopped dancing for good. Now Lydia says she'll divorce *me* if I ever come out of retirement." He gave her a droll look.

Melissa laughed because she knew she was expected to, but his humorous words left her with an uneasy, empty feeling.

"If you will not have an affair," Franchiese went on after a moment, his shrewd gaze sweeping around the room before it settled back on Melissa, "I will have you coach Dianne in *AfterImages.*"

"Dianne's going to cover my performances?" Melissa asked, not really surprised by the decision. Dianne Kelso was a promising young dancer from Los Angeles. Performing *AfterImages* could change her life . . . just as it had Melissa's.

AfterImages had made twenty-one-year-old Melissa Stewart an overnight sensation after sixteen years of hard work. It had also cost her Sean Culhane.

"She has the lyricism, but lacks the fire," Franchiese declared. "That, I hope, you can help her find." He smiled conspiratorially. "Who better to coach a role than the ballerina it was made on?"

"I'll do all I can," Melissa promised. "Although I always feel jealous when another dancer does that role."

"I would be disappointed if you did not. I made that dance for you. *AfterImages* will always be yours, Melissa. I know how much you gave to it." With that he patted her cheek paternally, then rose and moved away.

Melissa blinked, her eyes clouding as she tried to focus on the dancers in the room. Bruno Franchiese was wrong. He had no idea how much she had given that ballet.

"Wonderful," her mother had drawled sarcastically when Melissa, soaring with happiness, told her of her decision to accept Sean's proposal. "One week ago Franchiese hands you success on a silver platter and now you're ready to throw it back in his face!"

"I'm not!"

"You are!" Verna Stewart had been a pretty woman when she'd come to New York City more than two decades before full of small-town dreams of dancing on Broadway. Disillusionment and bitter dissatisfaction with her lot in life had destroyed that prettiness. "I didn't scrimp and save so you could run off and get married just when you're about to amount to something."

"Mama—" Melissa couldn't bear the hurt and anger in her mother's voice. She knew the sacrifices her mother had made. She knew that in some ways her career meant more to her mother than it did to her. "Mama, I'm not going to quit dancing just because I marry Sean. He understands—"

"That's what you think now, Melissa, but you wait and see. How understanding do you think he'll be when he realizes you have to spend twelve hours a day, six days a week, at the theater? How understanding do you think he'll be when you have to leave him and tour with the company?"

"We'll work it out." She had tried to fight down the insidious doubts her mother's words were stirring within her.

"And what about children? How are you going to work that out?"

"Children?"

"A man like Sean Culhane will want children, Melissa. And he'll want them soon. A dancer's life is very short. Getting yourself pregnant will make it even shorter. Practically nonexistent."

"I love him."

"If he loved you, he wouldn't force you into this."

"Force? Mama! I want to marry him!"

"If he loved you, he'd be willing to wait."

"Wait?"

"You say he wants to get married right away. Why the rush? And why now, only a few days after Franchiese gives you your big break?"

"I don't think—"

"Melissa, honey, I'm trying to save you from making the same mistake I did. I don't want you to waste your life, too. Tell Sean you want to wait until the debut of this new ballet...until the spring gala. If he accepts that, I'll admit I've been wrong about him. If he doesn't..."

Of course Sean hadn't accepted it. They'd quarreled bitterly and parted with painful finality. Melissa had had nowhere to go but back to the demanding discipline of the ballet. Dancing had been her lifeline, her painkiller. By the time she snapped out of her desperate drive for forgetfulness and realized she no longer had to work herself into exhaustion to be able to sleep, she'd achieved the success her mother wanted so badly.

And now, here she was, feeling as unfulfilled as a woman as she was incapacitated as a dancer.

"Well, for somebody who was supposed to be in traction, you look pretty good, sweetie," Laurette Fishkin commented airily, sliding gracefully into a split beside Melissa after class was dismissed. A hazel-eyed redhead, Laurette was the company flirt. Despite their very different temperaments, she and Melissa were fast friends.

"Traction?"

"Um-hm." Laurette searched through her tote bag and dug out a cigarette. She lighted it and inhaled deeply. While smoking was discouraged in the company, a number of dancers clung to the nicotine habit as a means of keeping their weight down. "When you didn't come to class for two days in a row, the grapevine reported you were in traction. And a full body cast. You know how it is."

Melissa did know how it was. When dancers weren't dancing, they were gossiping. "Sorry to disappoint everybody, but it's just my knee. I'm out for two months."

"Bo-oring," Laurette drawled. "What are you going to do with yourself?"

"Mr. Franchiese wants me to try coaching." She smiled mischievously. "He also suggested I have an affair."

Laurette snickered. "Well, just don't go hunting through the company for a lover. Speaking from personal experience, I can tell you that anybody worth looking at twice is either taken or gay or both. Except Yuri, of course."

"Of course." Laurette's unflattering assessment of the amatory prospects offered by the male members of the MBT was familiar to Melissa. She had been hearing variations on it for four years now.

The redhead pulled off one of her pink pointe shoes and began massaging her toes. She grimaced. "Look," she said, "I'm going over to Capezio's before my rehearsal starts. They're having a sale on leotards. Want to come?"

"Sure," Melissa nodded, welcoming the suggestion.

"Great. I'll go get changed."

"Ever notice how people stare at us?" Laurette asked sometime later as they walked out of the theater and onto the huge Lincoln Center plaza. She gave a coquettish smile to an attractive lawyer-type in a conservative gray suit.

"It's because we walk like ducks," Melissa told her, referring to the characteristic turned-out-toe walk that distinguished ballet dancers.

"Swans, sweetie," the redhead reproved her. "Franchiese's ballerinas move like swans, not ducks."

"Ummm." Melissa nodded absently, caught up, as she so often was, in admiration of the huge Marc Chagall murals that hung with bold beauty in the enormous glass windows of the upper level of the Metropolitan Opera House.

"Not that I mind being stared at," Laurette chattered on. "In fact—" She broke off abruptly, coming to a dead stop and grabbing Melissa's arm. "Now, that is something worth staring at!" she exclaimed yearningly.

"Laurette, what are you talking—oh, no!" Melissa swayed, feeling as though she'd been jolted by an electric shock.

Sean Culhane was perched comfortably on the rim of the circular fountain in the middle of the plaza, his long, powerfully muscled legs stretched out in front of him. There was a coiled-spring quality to his casual posture; he was relaxed yet watchful.

He was wearing battered running shoes and well-worn tight-fitting jeans that emphasized the strongly masculine lines of his lower body. He had on a pale blue work shirt, which was partially unbuttoned, revealing a triangle of tanned hair-rough chest. A navy-blue sweater was tied nonchalantly around his shoulders.

The golden autumn sun burnished the sensual planes of his face and highlighted the palest blond strands of his wind-ruffled hair. Sean disarranged his tawny thatch even more when he pulled off the mirrored sunglasses that were hiding his eyes and shoved them up on top of his head.

"He's looking at us," Laurette breathed. "And now he's getting up. Oh, Melissa—Melissa?" She glanced away from Sean long enough to see the distress on her friend's face. "Do you know him?"

Melissa took a deep breath, fighting the urge to turn and run. Sean was approaching them with long, lithe strides, his eyes fixed on her compellingly. "Yes," she admitted quietly. "I know him."

"I thought I'd find you here," Sean said as he reached them. His gaze moved angrily over Melissa's taut, slender body. "What's wrong with you?" he demanded. "Dave Goldberg told you to stay out for two months. You're back after two days! Forget physical therapy for your knee, Melissa. You should have your head examined!"

Her chin came up. "And hello to you, too, Sean," she snapped, her eyes flashing icy fire.

"You took class today, didn't you?" he accused.

"What if I did?"

"What the hell are you trying to prove? That you're so dedicated to dancing you'll cripple yourself?" His powerful hands closed over her fragile shoulders and he shook her once. "Is that it?" His grip tightened for a moment, then his palms slid possessively down her arms, lingering as though he were reluctant to release her.

Melissa jerked herself free, glaring at him. "What are you trying to prove?" she threw back at him.

Sean got his temper under control with a visible effort. "Did you take class today?" he snapped.

"I—" Melissa started to inform him it was no business of his, when she realized there was more than anger in his face. Concern, deep and undisguised, shadowed the depths of his green-gold eyes. Not quite believing she was reading the look correctly, Melissa stared up at him searchingly for a long moment. She only vaguely registered that Laurette was still standing next to her, avidly drinking in every detail.

"Are you . . . worried about me, Sean?" she asked uncertainly.

"Would it be so surprising if I were?"

She hesitated. "I—I did go to class," she said finally.

"Damn!"

"But only to watch!" she added hastily, taken aback by the force of his temper. "I had to."

"You had to sit around a rehearsal hall and torture yourself over dancing?"

That's better than sitting around my apartment torturing myself over you!

The bitter retort sprang to her lips unbidden and she just barely managed to choke it back. It was with a sense of shock that she realized there was more than a little truth to the statement.

"I'm still on the MBT payroll," she said as evenly as she could. "I had a responsibility to put in an appearance. You used to show up at the stadium even if you weren't playing, didn't you?"

"Sean Culhane!" Laurette blurted out unexpectedly. *"That's* who you are! My God, I had no idea you were so gorgeous in real life. My three brothers used to rave about your arm or something." She flashed an inviting smile. "Now, I wouldn't know about your arm, but the rest—"

"Laurette!" Melissa made an exasperated sound somewhere between a groan and a laugh.

Sean grinned appreciatively, his very potent masculine charm coming into play as he turned to the redhead. Melissa knew from personal experience just how overwhelming the Culhane brand of sex appeal could be.

"You must be Laurette Fishkin," Sean said pleasantly.

"That's right," Laurette affirmed, clearly flattered. "But how did you know?"

"Any friend of Melissa's is a friend of mine," he replied, his intonation giving the clichéd remark a very intimate undertone. Melissa suppressed a desire to slug him when she saw Laurette's eyebrows go up in arch understanding. While the redhead hadn't been with the company during her affair with Sean, she'd probably heard gossip about it. This little confrontation would be on the grapevine within hours.

"Didn't you say you had to get to Capezio's, Laurette?" Melissa prodded. The time for subtlety—if there had ever been one—was long gone. She gave Sean a pseudo-sweet smile. "They're having a sale on practice clothes."

"Oh, I can go there by myself," Laurette declared

blithely, her hazel eyes sparkling. "You stay here, Melissa." She slanted a flirtatiously encouraging glance at Sean. "After all, there's more to life than trying on tights."

"Laurette—"

The redhead picked up her tote bag, slinging it over her angular shoulder. "So nice to have met you, Sean. Have fun, kids!" She wagged her fingers in farewell.

"Laurette!" Melissa exclaimed.

"Don't forget what Franchiese told you!" Laurette called over her shoulder as she walked away.

"She seemed very friendly," Sean observed blandly.

Melissa whirled on him, infuriated by the gleam of amusement in his eyes and the deepening of the dimple at the corner of his mouth. "I suppose you think this is all very funny!" she flared.

"Former quarterbacks have weird senses of humor."

"You thought what happened Tuesday was funny, too, didn't you?"

"Tuesday?" He looked puzzled.

"You were laughing when you walked away from me."

"Oh, that." He chuckled, hooking his thumbs into the belt loops of his jeans. The movement tugged the form-fitting denim tight across his blatantly masculine anatomy.

"Yes, that!"

"I was laughing at the idea that you actually thought having an unlisted number would stop me from getting in touch with you. You know me better than that, Melissa." He raised one brow, dropping his voice caressingly, as though reminding her of just how well she knew him—and he her. "By the way, what did Franchiese tell you?"

"Franchiese—"

"Was it something about sex?"

"Sex!" It came out far louder than she had intended. Melissa flushed with embarrassment as she drew a disapproving look from a middle-aged matron who was at that moment strolling by. "Not all men have their minds in their jockstraps," she informed Sean through clenched teeth.

"True," he laughed. "But the one time I talked to your esteemed director, he told me he thought our sex life had done wonders for your dancing."

Outrageous as the comment was, Melissa could easily imagine Bruno Franchiese saying just such a thing. What she couldn't figure out was when he might have met Sean. She put that puzzle out of her mind with a toss of her head. "What are you doing here?" she asked irritably.

"Ah, time for the instant replay."

"I beg your pardon?"

"That's the same question you asked me two days ago at the sports clinic. I'm afraid the answer's the same, too. I've been waiting for you."

"I don't believe this!"

"I told you I wanted to see you again." The look in his eyes warned her suddenly that he wanted to do a lot more than just see her. His gaze traveled boldly to her mouth, down to her breasts, and back up to her mouth. Melissa was appalled to feel a responsive tightening of her nipples and a fluttering heat lower down in her body.

"Well, I don't want to see you," she got out breathlessly, and started to turn away. He caught her arm and spun her back.

"Melissa, I'm sorry," he said quickly, his expression disarmingly apologetic. "Really, I am. I didn't show up here intending to put your back up...or to come on to you." He smiled ruefully. "Some things just happen."

"Not if you don't let them, they don't."

He let go of her, raising his hands in a gesture of surrender. Even through two layers of cloth she could still feel the tingling imprint of his fingers on her skin. "Okay, okay. Hands off." He paused, gauging her mood carefully. "Look, Melissa, I have a proposition for you.

A strictly professional proposition."

She watched him narrowly, wondering what he was up to. "I can't dance, remember? I've been, ah, benched. Sidelined. Sent to the showers."

"I know, sweetheart." Compassionate understanding flickered across his face. "This proposition doesn't involve your actually dancing. Have you given much thought to what you're going to do with yourself for the next two months?"

Melissa gave a mirthless laugh. "That's hardly an original question. I'm not sure yet. Mr. Franchiese has asked me to do some coaching . . . that's it for now."

"You don't have any other commitments?"

"Sean, what are you driving at?"

"All right. A friend of mine runs a youth center uptown — way uptown. It offers a bunch of activities aimed at keeping younger kids off the streets and out of trouble after school. My friend's been holding an ad hoc dance class a couple of days a week as part of the program. The problem is, Rita doesn't have any real background in dance."

"Rita? Your friend is a woman?"

"Yeah. She's a very special lady."

"I see." Melissa felt as though she'd been kicked. She saw the way his features softened when he mentioned this Rita. *What did you expect?* she asked herself furiously. *Of course he has a "special lady" in his life!*

"This place is nothing fancy," he went on. "There's a bar for exercises, but no mirrors. The center has enough problems with vandalized windows. The kids bring in their own records to use for accompaniment. One of the companies I'm doing endorsements for makes dance gear. We got a good deal on leotards, tights, and shoes from them."

"You want me to teach these children . . . at this center?"

"Right. You've worked with kids before, haven't you?

In the city's Dance-in-the-Schools program?"

Melissa looked surprised. She'd begun to donate her time to that project only two years before. "Yes, but how—"

"This will be the same sort of thing," he interrupted. "Frankly some of the kids in Rita's little group don't know right from left, and their ideas about dancing are more boogie than ballet. But having someone like you, even for a few weeks, could make a big difference in their lives." He gave her a persuasive smile, his appeal unexpectedly intense.

He must care for this Rita very much, Melissa thought with a pang. That's why this is so important to him. He wants to do something special for his "special lady."

"How—how often would this be?" she asked.

"Twice a week, after school. There are about two dozen or so kids coming on a regular basis. Rita's even recruited a boy for the class."

She nodded slowly. "Sean . . . if I—it could only be for the two months I'm out. After that I'll have to devote all my time to getting back into performance condition."

"I understand that."

"Well, I don't want to start something and then have the children feel as though I'm walking out on them."

"No problem. You can explain the situation up front." He paused. "I'm not trying to force you into this. If you don't want—"

"No," she interrupted firmly. "I'd like to do it."

"Terrific! Let's go then." He took her hand as though it were the most natural thing in the world to do. Their fingers intertwined intimately.

Melissa didn't try to pull away. She didn't want to. Having her hand clasped in his felt utterly right. She did, however, refuse to budge from where she was standing.

"Let's go where?" she questioned suspiciously.

"The youth center. I just remembered there happens to be a dance class scheduled for this afternoon."

"You just remembered?"

"That's right," he confirmed with mock innocence. "This is the perfect opportunity for you to, ah, audition your students."

"Scout the rookies, you mean," she amended with a quicksilver smile, finding herself more amused than offended by his unabashed manipulation of the situation.

"You really do read the sports pages, don't you?" Hand in hand they began to walk toward the curb.

"I read them enough to spot a quarterback sneak." She halted suddenly, a thought occurring to her. "Isn't this the middle of the workday for you? Aren't you supposed to be showing off track shoes or teaching aerobics?"

He laughed aloud at her flippant description of his business activities. In addition to sportscasting and doing celebrity endorsements, Sean was involved in a number of fitness-related investment ventures.

"I'm a free agent these days, Twinkletoes," he replied. Her heart skipped a beat at the use of the old nickname. "That means I can give myself time off when I want to."

"Is your friend—Rita—expecting us?"

"I did mention something to her about the possibility of our dropping by."

"I see. You were that sure I'd say yes?"

His brows rose in sardonic emphasis, but his eyes were serious and steady. "I said I mentioned the possibility, Melissa, that's all. But I was sure you'd say yes. If not to me, then to work that involves your beloved dance. Now, shall we go?"

CHAPTER THREE

THE YOUTH CENTER was much as Sean had described it. Yet as run-down as the place was, it had an aura of positive energy and hope about it.

"One flight up," he told her as they entered the two-story graffiti-covered building.

When they reached the second floor Melissa looked around, orienting herself. The room was surprisingly large and airy. An assortment of brightly colored posters decorated the drab walls. About two dozen youngsters were present, some sprawled on the floor, others prancing about restlessly, and a few stretching their limbs with careless flexibility. The youngest appeared to be a pixie-faced black girl who was twirling around in one corner with dizzying skill. The oldest was an amber-skinned boy of about fourteen who had an intense and defiant air.

"*Querido!*" This affectionate exclamation came from

a vibrantly beautiful woman in her late twenties. Although casually—almost sloppily—dressed, she radiated hot-blooded sensuality. Her Latin heritage was evident in her olive complexion and flashing dark eyes. Looking at her, Melissa felt a sharp stab of jealousy. This, obviously, was Sean's "special lady."

Grinning, Sean accepted, then returned, the woman's exuberant hug and kiss. "Now, this is the kind of reception I like," he said. "Rita, meet Melissa Stewart. Melissa, Ms. Rita Perez."

"I'm glad to meet you at last," Rita said, smiling.

"I—" The woman's unforced warmth took Melissa by surprise. She responded with a smile of her own, conscious that Sean was watching her. "I'm glad to meet you, too, Ms. Perez."

"Rita, please! And I hope you don't mind if I call you Melissa. I feel as though I know you already."

"You do?"

"Rita's a ballet fan," Sean cut in smoothly. Melissa saw a curious look pass between him and the attractive social worker. "As a matter of fact, she was at *Giselle* on Sunday."

"That's right," Rita confirmed quickly. "I had no idea you were injured until Sean—" She broke off, flashing her smile again. "I hope it's nothing serious."

"It's just a problem with my knee," Melissa said. There was something odd going on, but she couldn't quite put her finger on what it was. "It hurts only when I dance," she added wryly. "Which is why I'm here. Sean—Sean told me about the classes you hold. I'd like to help out—at least for the next six or eight weeks. If you can use me."

"Use you?" Rita gave a throaty laugh. "We'll work you to death if you let us. When can you start?"

The woman's eagerness was infectious. "Right now, I suppose," Melissa answered.

"Wonderful! Let me introduce you to the gang." Be-

fore Melissa could react further, Rita waved Sean off
into a corner, took her by the arm, and led her to the
center of the room. She clapped her hands loudly several
times, then let loose with a shrill whistle.

"Bueno," she declared as the children settled into
relative quiet. "We have a special guest today—"

"El León," one girl volunteered, setting off an explosion of giggles. It was obvious Sean's appeal wasn't
lost on the preteen set.

"No, he's here too much to be special," Rita answered, casting a cheeky grin at Melissa. "This is our
special guest. Her name is Melissa Stewart and she is a
real dancer. A Ballerina."

There was an impressed chorus of *oohs* and *aahs* from
the children, and Melissa found herself the focus of
roughly twenty-four pairs of eyes. The youthful scrutiny
went on for nearly a minute.

"Are you going to dance for us?" someone finally
piped up hopefully.

Melissa smiled ruefully. "Well, actually, I was hoping
you'd dance for me," she said. "I've hurt my knee and
I'm supposed to take it easy. But Ms. Perez has said it's
okay if I help with your class. I'd like that."

"What knee?" This came from the littlest girl.

"My right one."

"Didja break it?"

Melissa suppressed a wince. "No, lucky for me. One
of the ways dancers keep from injuring themselves is to
warm up, just like you've probably seen athletes do on
television. So, why don't we start with some warm-up
exercises?"

After improvising a series of bends and stretches for
the children, Melissa taught them some very basic dance
steps, complimenting and correcting them as she went
along. At one point, caught up in the spirit of things,
she slipped off her shoes and danced through a simple
combination, ending with a smooth pirouette.

In the final minutes she divided the class into small groups and let them make up their own dances to the driving beat of a popular rock song. All the students threw themselves into the challenge with enthusiasm. Several of them—particularly the intense teenage boy she'd noted earlier—showed a definite aptitude.

At the end of the session the children burst into spontaneous applause. Melissa found their appreciation very sweet. Afterward they clustered around her, asking questions and vying for her attention. Rita Perez finally came to the rescue, but not before Melissa had promised to come again on Tuesday.

"You're a hit, Twinkletoes," Sean said, coming over to her.

"She's more than that, *chico*," Rita declared, having firmly shooed the remaining stragglers away. "You're a miracle, Melissa. You actually had all of them doing just what you told them to do!"

"I've taken classes with enough tyrannical dance teachers to know the technique." Melissa smiled modestly. "You've got to be a cross between Vince Lombardi at half-time and Attila the Hun commanding the horde."

"Whatever," Rita laughed, tossing her head. She slipped an arm about Sean's waist, slanting a flirtatious look up at him. "Sean, I don't know how I'm going to thank you for bringing Melissa to us."

"Oh, I'm sure you'll think of something," he returned, his lips quirking. Melissa's heart dropped at the banter. "One thing, though. She's supposed to be taking it easy. That crack about working her to death—"

"As if I would, Sean Culhane!"

"Control the Latin temper, Rita. It's the dancing demon I'm worried about." He gave Melissa an assessing look. "That little combination was very impressive, sweetheart, but I don't think pirouettes are on the approved list of activities for you right now."

"I did only one," she protested. "And on my left leg."

"With you, pirouettes are addictive. Once you get started, you can't stop."

"It wasn't even a very good turn," Melissa groused. "My close to fifth was sloppy."

Sean shook his head despairingly. "You see what I mean, Rita?" he asked. "Just try to keep her off her knee and out of trouble while she's here, okay?"

A week passed before Melissa saw Sean again. As the days went by she found herself thinking increasingly of him and of what they had had together five years before. She ended up drifting off into erotic daydreams at the most inopportune times—during an *AfterImages* coaching session with Dianne Kelso and Rex Castleberry, for example.

The memories closed in most seductively at night as she went to bed, alone. The control she consciously exerted over herself loosened as she slipped toward sleep, and a throbbing hunger grew within her body in response to her subconscious yearnings.

For years she'd lost herself in the physical demands of the dance. She'd considered herself a very cool-blooded girl before she'd met Sean. Shy except in a performance or practice situation, she'd had little inclination and even less time for flirtations and dating. Sean, with his ardent courtship, had awakened the sensual nature that slumbered beneath her inexperience. He had reveled in her innocent responsiveness, teaching her the pleasures she had been created to give...and to receive.

She had not been prepared for the sheer ache of frustration she'd felt after they broke up. Yet she had forced herself through it, discovering that the passage of time dimmed and dampened the restless urge of passion.

Or so she'd foolishly believed.

"Poor Sean," Rita commented the following Thursday as she helped Melissa sort through a stack of records in preparation for the afternoon's class.

"Why do you say that?" Melissa asked.

"When he quit football he thought he was going to be able to settle down. Instead, he's had to travel more than ever. On business. I thought he sounded distinctly homesick on the phone yesterday."

Melissa made a neutral sound, staring blankly at an album cover. "You spoke to him yesterday?" she asked casually, trying to control the resentment she felt over the fact that Rita had heard from Sean and she had not.

"Just for a few moments. Don't worry, though. I told him you were being careful with your knee."

"Thank you."

"*De nada.*" Rita shrugged. "After all, we women have to stick together. Your knee is doing all right, isn't it?" She glanced questioningly at Melissa's right leg.

Partly because she wanted to satisfy the children's image of a "ballerina," and partly because she felt most comfortable in practice clothes, Melissa had decided to wear her usual rehearsal outfit of a black leotard and pink tights to the youth center. She'd added a pair of old black leg warmers and knotted a pullover sweater around her narrow waist as well. Only the neat wrappings of an Ace bandage around her knee hinted at anything out of the ordinary.

"It seems to be doing fine," she replied, absently readjusting one of the pins holding her hair in a bun.

"That's good." The other woman watched with fascinated amusement as Melissa unzipped her canvas tote bag and extracted a sweatshirt. Melissa pulled it on over everything else. Rather than making her appear bulky, the various layers of clothing served only to emphasize the fragile elegance of her body. "Do all dancers look like you?" Rita asked irrepressibly.

Melissa laughed. "You mean, do all dancers dress like bag ladies? Only at class and rehearsals. It's mostly to keep our muscles warm."

"I guarantee you half the kids will be coming to class

layered to the eyebrows before the month is over," Rita declared. "I, on the other hand, am not about to try any additional layers anywhere!"

"But you have a terrific figure," Melissa assured her honestly, wistfully comparing Rita's all-female curves to her own slight form.

"Well, I do all right," Rita conceded, winking.

The class went very well. The teenage boy Melissa had picked out continued to show great promise. She'd learned his name was Tonio and that his air of defiance was a defense against the heckling he took because of his desire to dance.

She ended the lesson once again by allowing the children to improvise their own routines. Afterward, a group of youngsters crowded around her, brimming with questions.

"Does it take long to get to be a ballerina?" one of the girls wanted to know.

"Well, you have to start when you're little and work very hard at it. Sometimes, even that's not enough."

"How long've you been dancing?"

"I've been studying about twenty years."

There were exclamations of astonishment at this.

"Wow, you must be really old!"

Melissa made a droll face. "I'm twenty-six." *A dancer's life is very short.* The words reverberated inside her skull.

"Did you always want to do ballet?"

It was an innocent enough question, but it gave Melissa pause. She could barely remember a time when she hadn't been dancing. "I didn't know about it when I started," she said truthfully. "My mother took me to my first class. She wanted me to be a ballerina."

"Was she one?"

"No . . . she came to New York to become a dancer, though."

"What happened?"

"She had me, for one thing. She had to stop being a dancer and be my mother instead." She smiled, shutting her mind to the echo of her mother's voice repeating over and over how much she had given up for her only daughter.

"Can't ballerinas be mothers?"

"They can if they want," a male voice said steadily.

"Sean!" Melissa turned, a sense of relief and surprised delight filling her.

"Hi." He was the picture of a successful businessman in his charcoal-gray vested suit, white shirt, and burgundy and black tie. He grinned at her with lazy assurance, his eyes running over her in leisurely assessment. "I thought the teacher was supposed to keep the kids after class, not the other way around."

Although clearly disappointed at the interruption, the children responded to the hint in Sean's teasing voice and scampered off.

"They can't get enough of you, hmmm?" he asked, walking over to her.

The room seemed to shrink as he moved closer. Feigning an indifference she was far from feeling, Melissa lifted one leg and stripped off the knitted leg warmer. She shrugged her response to his question, wishing she weren't quite so aware of his physical proximity.

"It's an understandable problem," he drawled. "I never could either."

Startled, she looked up and nearly lost her balance. His hands closed around her slim hips in the same split-second, steadying her. The thin fabric of her leotard offered no protection against the warmth of his palms. That warmth triggered a melting heat in the lower part of her body.

"Sean, please—" Her wide gray eyes were on level with his broad chest. She tilted her head back slightly, her long slender neck arching in pale vulnerability. The baggy collar of her sweatshirt gapped, revealing the frantic pulsing of the vein at the side of her throat.

"Please—" she whispered.

He let her go. "Sorry," he said tersely.

She managed a crooked smile, uncertain of the reason for his apology. "Mr. Franchiese once told me I was a natural for the Rose Adagio in *Sleeping Beauty* because of my balancés. I think he'd take it back if he'd seen me just now." She paused to pull off the other leg warmer, bracing herself against the wall this time as she cast about for a safe topic of conversation. "I—did you have a pleasant trip? Rita mentioned you were out of town."

"It was more profitable than pleasant. I was going to call, but I didn't have your number. You really aren't in the book."

"*Of course* I'm not." She felt an absurd thrill of pleasure at his words. So he had been thinking about her! With an unconsciously provocative wriggle, she pulled off her sweatshirt, then bent and stuffed it into her bag.

"You aren't going out like that, are you?" he asked. "Those legs of yours will cause a riot."

She glanced down at herself. "I beg your pardon?"

"It always used to amaze me that the more you put on, the sexier you got."

Melissa lowered her lashes, veiling her eyes. Her pulse was pounding erratically. "I—I think I'd better go change," she decided breathlessly and moved away, feeling his jungle-cat eyes focused on her back.

She returned five minutes later in jeans, boots, and a white Victorian-style blouse she'd discovered in a Greenwich Village thrift shop. Her hair, freed from its confining bun, tumbled in glossy darkness to the small of her back. She found Sean engaged in conversation with Rita Perez. The harmony between the two was evident, even from across the room. Melissa experienced a flash of anger—partly for Rita, whom she was beginning to like very much, and partly for herself. Why was Sean flirting with her when he was so clearly involved with another woman?

"Well, I guess I'll be heading downtown," she announced. "I'll see you again on Tuesday, Rita."

"We can go together," Sean said. "I had my cab wait."

"No, that's not necessary," Melissa protested. "I'm sure you and Rita—"

"We've got plenty of time to get together," Rita cut in with a breezy gesture. She glanced inquiringly at Sean. "Are we still on for the weekend?"

"Have I ever let you down?"

"Well . . ."

"Come on, Melissa. Let's get away before she starts to dredge up my sordid past. *Adiós, chiquita.*"

"Hasta luego, León mío. Bye-bye, Melissa."

The ride downtown was a stop-start affair due to late-afternoon traffic. For the first few minutes they chatted about inconsequential things. Then, abruptly, Sean changed the subject.

"It isn't easy for you to talk about your mother, is it?" he asked.

Melissa stiffened, twisting a lock of hair around one finger. "I—I don't know what you mean."

"The questions the kids were asking you back at the center. I could see it hurt. You never talked about her much when we were together, either."

She looked at him sharply, her gray eyes shadowed and faintly accusatory. "I never had the feeling my mother was a topic you wanted to discuss."

"I want to know about you, Melissa. Your mother is a big part of your life."

"My mother's dead."

"And my father died when I was eighteen. But a lot of who I am and what I do is still influenced by him."

"You never liked her, did you?"

"Your mother? No more than she liked me," he answered honestly.

She turned her gaze to the window, her hair swinging forward to hide her face. After drawing a deep breath she spoke slowly. "Look, I know you have some idea that my mother forced me into dancing and kept me there, but that's not the way it was. I wanted it, too."

"As badly as she did?"

"I—"

"And what about your father? In all the time we were together five years ago, you spoke of him only once."

She'd told Sean her father had died before she was born, leaving her mother a nineteen-year-old widow with a baby on the way. That wasn't the truth.

"My father deserted my mother when she was pregnant with me," she said suddenly, leaning her forehead against the glass. "I—I'm not even sure they were ever married." It was something she had never confided to anyone.

There was a long silence, shattered only when their driver began honking his horn at the car in front of him. Melissa felt Sean's hand close over her shoulder, gently forcing her to turn back toward him. While she didn't resist the pressure, she did keep her head stubbornly down for a moment, afraid of what she might see in his face if she looked.

"I wish you'd told me that before."

Her eyes sought his searchingly, but his expression was carefully controlled. "Why?" she asked. "What possible difference could it have made?"

"It might have helped me understand you better."

She shook her head. "I'm a dancer. That's all you have to understand."

"Oh, there's a lot more to understand about you than that." He regarded her with unnerving intensity for a few moments, then smiled slowly, the fine network of lines coming into play at the corners of his eyes. "Just as there's more to life than trying on tights, as your friend Laurette said the other day."

They spent the remainder of the ride in silence. Melissa was lost in her own thoughts, somewhat shaken by what she had revealed. Sean seemed preoccupied as well.

She was so bemused that she did not immediately grasp the fact that Sean got out and paid the cabbie when the taxi arrived in front of her building. By the time she realized what was going on, the cab had already sped away and Sean was politely holding the entrance door open for her.

"What do you think you're doing?" she demanded.

"I'm coming up to your apartment to wait while you change so I can take you to dinner," he answered mildly.

"No!"

"No what?"

"You can't come up to my apartment."

"You used to come up to mine," he reminded her.

"That was—and where did you get the idea I'm going to let you take me to dinner?"

"We both have to eat."

"I have other plans." She lied stiffly.

"Like what? Washing your hair?"

She glared at him. "Did you ever consider that maybe I don't *want* to have dinner with you?"

"Not for a second, sweetheart," he replied pleasantly.

Melissa made a sound of exasperated disbelief.

"Is that an acceptance I hear?"

Her brain was shrieking "no!" The word that came out of her mouth was exactly the opposite. "But only if we go to an Italian restaurant," she added, seeking to mitigate her capitulation least a little.

"You still have a passion for pasta, hmmm? Well, who am I to leave a lady's basic hungers unsatisfied?"

"Come on," Melissa instructed ungraciously.

Once they reached her third-floor apartment it took her several moments to search through her tote bag and locate her key. She inserted it into her door with a practiced jiggle and gave the knob a shove. Sticky locks were among the minor eccentricities featured in her modest building.

"My place is very small," she commented, still trying to rotate the key.

"I don't take up much room."

"I have a cat."

"I do take up more room than a cat," he conceded. "Do you need a hand with the door?" He leaned forward helpfully. Whether by accident or design, their bodies brushed together briefly. The fleeting contact made Melissa aware, once again, of his hard male strength and his innate, but carefully leashed, physical power.

"No!" Melissa shied away. "Thank you," she tacked on quickly, then breathed a deep sigh of relief as the lock finally gave with an audible click. "It's not much," she declared, opening the door. "But it's home."

The housing situation being what it was in New York City, Melissa counted herself extremely fortunate to have found her small but comfortable one-bedroom apartment. Blessed with a pleasant expanse of windows and done up in a serene combination of cream, green, and blue, it offered a relaxing haven from the pressures of big-city life.

Melissa flipped on the foyer light as she walked in ahead of Sean. She heard the door close behind her. "Watch out," she warned with a trace of whimsy. "My cat is attack-trained."

"I think he needs a refresher course," Sean commented as Melissa heard a familiar "me-row." She turned to see Sean stooped down to scratch an all-too-willing Nijinsky's fluffy head.

Despite his distinguished name, Nijinsky was an undistinguished cat of unknown breeding. He was also a creature of capricious independence who sometimes appeared to think that he, not Melissa, was in charge of the apartment.

"Be careful." She had very few visitors, and Nijinsky tended to react to strangers with hostility. No telling what he might do next.

"I think he likes me," Sean grinned, giving the cat a final tickle and then straightening up. Nijinsky was purring like an unmuffled motor.

"Maybe he senses a kindred spirit," Melissa suggested dryly, mildly irritated with her cat. The last time she'd invited a man in—a very charming pianist who occasionally filled in as an accompanist at MBT rehearsals— Nijinsky had greeted him with hisses and unsheathed claws.

"Could be."

Melissa glanced around. With time weighing heavily on her hands, she'd embarked on an orgy of housecleaning. The place was virtually spotless. "I—I don't really have anything to offer you," she said awkwardly. "There's some mineral water in the refrigerator and some fruit juice."

"I'll survive," he cut in easily, unbuttoning his jacket and vest and thrusting his hands deep into his trouser pockets. "Why don't you go change? Take a bath if you want. I'm in no hurry."

Feeling strangely uneasy, Melissa nodded and exited into her bedroom, shutting the door firmly behind her.

"You're crazy for doing this, Melissa Stewart," she whispered to herself as she swiftly stripped down. Wrapping herself in her sea-green terry-cloth robe, she padded silently into the bathroom.

She showered quickly, rubbing her slender body with lotion after she dried off. Then, clipping her dark hair haphazardly back off her face, she put on some makeup.

Her skin was pale and poreless. MBT dancers were constantly being warned against exposure to the sun. The idea of a tanned Swan Queen was anathema to Bruno Franchiese. Melissa smoothed on a sheer layer of ivory foundation and brushed a light rose pink blush on her high cheekbones. Her mind wandered unsettlingly to the contrast between her fair, untouched complexion and Sean's sun-bronzed one. Five years ago she'd discovered that he was the same healthy golden color all over. She wondered if he still . . .

She gave a hiss of frustration at her wayward imagination, hating her lack of control. Her fingers trembled ever so slightly as she showered her eyelids with a subtle gray-violet that lent a smoky, sultry quality to her expression. A skillful application of black kohl and glossy black mascara made her eyes look huge.

After briefly debating about whether or not to put her hair up, she unpinned it and brushed it free. Wearing it long and loose might not be the most sophisticated style in the world, but she took pride in its raven-wing shininess and enjoyed the silken swing of it over her shoulders.

Besides, a little voice inside her head piped up annoyingly, *Sean always asked you to wear it down.*

After misting herself with a delicate floral fragrance, Melissa switched off the bathroom light and went back into her bedroom. She'd already decided what she was going to wear. Donning a pair of ultrasheer pantyhose and an outrageously expensive set of ecru satin and lace underwear she'd given herself for Christmas, she crossed to the closet and pulled out an elegantly simple dress of amethyst silk. High-necked and long-sleeved, with a wide matching belt, it was trimmed with trapunto embroidery at the collar, hem, and cuffs.

It had only one minor flaw, a flaw Melissa didn't remember until it was too late.

The zipper in back was tricky, to say the least.

"Damn!" Melissa exclaimed as she felt it stick about halfway up. Twisting, she tried to get enough leverage to pull it free, then realized the thing had apparently snagged on the delicate fabric of her slip for good measure.

Steeling herself against hearing a telltale rip, she tried to ease the dress up, hoping to wriggle out of it. She quickly discovered the zipper had closed just far enough to make such a maneuver impossible.

Melissa grimaced, silently berating herself. Much as she disliked it, there was only one thing to do.

Mustering her dignity, she slipped her feet into a pair of strappy black sandals, stuck a few necessities into a matching envelope bag, and searched through her drawers until she located her cobwebby black shawl. Tossing her hair back, she tilted her chin and returned to the living room.

Sean rose slowly from her couch as she came in, his eyes scanning her appreciatively.

"If Gershwin had seen you looking like that, he probably would have called it *Rhapsody in Purple* . . . not *Blue*."

Melissa drew a shaky breath, setting down her shawl and handbag. "Yes . . . well, thank you," she returned. "But I have a small problem. My—the zipper's stuck." She made a wry face. "Could you—?"

"With pleasure, Twinkletoes. Turn around."

The minute she felt the sweep of his fingers over the back of her shoulders as he casually brushed her long hair out of the way, she knew she'd made a terrible mistake. The clean masculine scent of him assailed her nostrils, triggering a host of memories. It seemed that every nerve in her body was acutely and individually signaling its awareness of his nearness.

"You still have the most exquisite skin I've ever seen," he said. His warm breath fanned caressingly across the nape of her neck as he traced a path down her back from the indentation between her shoulder blades to the point where the zipper had jammed.

"Sean—" She clenched her hands, her nails biting into her palms, trying to ignore the quiver that ran through her.

"What have we here?" he murmured thoughtfully. He placed one hand, fingers splayed, at the base of her spine, pulling the zipper track tight. "Let's see—"

Melissa knew there was no way he could not be aware of the physical reactions he was stirring within her. While Sean had proven to be a demanding, virile lover in their time together, he had always been tenderly sensitive to her responses as well. There had been moments when she'd felt he knew her body better than she did.

She felt the material give as he worked the zipper free of its snag. A moment later he gave a soft grunt of satisfaction and tugged the tab upward in one smooth movement.

The next thing she knew, he had pressed his mouth to the naked skin at the side of her throat just above the neckline of the dress. She bit her lip, choking back a moan as his warm, moist tongue flicked her flesh.

"Se-Sean—"

Before she could protest further, he turned her around and covered her parted lips with his own. He drank in the taste of her with the pleasurable deliberation of a connoisseur.

His questing tongue ran slickly over the smooth barrier of her teeth, persuading her to yield him more intimate access. Teasing and tempting, he took her surrender with lingering expertise, then began to coax something more from her.

Melissa made no conscious decision to kiss him back, but suddenly that was just what she was doing. Her tongue met his shyly, and as the hot, hungry flavor of him flooded into her, the hesitation vanished. Arching up, she locked her arms around his neck, her fingers seeking the crisp thicket of tawny hair at his nape. She felt light-headed and dizzy, with the room spinning around her as though she'd done too many pirouettes.

Even with several layers of clothing separating them, she was aware of the taut play of his muscles and the throbbing pressure of his masculinity. They were the center of her universe, rousing her to aching, yearning life. The physical affinity had always been strong between them; even after all this time the elemental call of body to body was almost irresistible.

Almost, but not quite.

Afterward Melissa was never certain what had triggered her resistance. The drugging expertise of his loveplay undermined her inhibitions as though they had never existed. She heard herself whimpering in soft response as his left hand slid up her torso and closed over her breast.

The nipple stiffened to a taut point. Sean tantalized the sensitive crest with the ball of his thumb, creating an almost painfully erotic sensation. The wispy layers of her bra and slip and the fine fabric of her dress did little to interfere with his knowing exploration.

He deepened the kiss, the skilled thrust of his tongue becoming more demanding. The movement of it signaled his intentions quite clearly. To give in to those intentions would be so blissfully easy. . . .

She shuddered and began to stiffen. *What was she doing?*

"Sean, no—" She tried to pull back, twisting her face away from him.

"What—" His voice was hoarse; the gold in his eyes glittered alarmingly.

"Please, don't. *Please*. I'm not ready for this!"

CHAPTER FOUR

S<small>EAN LET HER</small> go so abruptly, she had to take a stumbling step backward before she regained her balance.

"You're not ready?" he echoed. "If you were any more ready, you'd be going up in flames!"

Melissa couldn't deny it. The quivering in her thighs, the aroused press of delicate breasts against the bodice of her dress, the hectic sexual flush on her cheeks, all betrayed her. It was both heaven and hell to find that they still had the power to move each other in such an earth-shattering fashion.

"When you asked me to dinner I didn't know you were intending to have me for an appetizer," she declared, her voice brittle.

"Hardly that, sweetheart. You'd be a feast to a starving man."

"Starv—" Her long-lashed gray eyes widened. "What about Rita?" she demanded.

He regarded her silently for a moment. The molten heat of desire she had seen in his eyes cooled as he got himself back under control. "What about her?"

"I like Rita."

"So do I."

"Well, then . . . how can you—" she gestured agitatedly. "You and I—we can't—"

"Melissa, what the hell does Rita Perez have to do with us?"

She stared at him in disbelief. Sean had a great many faults, but emotional game-playing wasn't one of them.

"I like Rita!" she repeated. "I can't . . . with you . . . not if—" She shook her head. "Don't you *see?*"

His brows went up sharply. "Time out. You think I've got something going with Rita?" There was a curious tremor in his voice.

"Don't you?" Even to her own ears the question sounded plaintive.

The strong, clean line of his jaw worked for a moment, signifying some type of inner struggle. "Is Rita the real reason you stopped me?" he countered.

A fine line creased the skin between her brows at his apparent evasion. "I don't—" She bit her lip, looking away from his searching gaze for a moment. Rita Perez had been the farthest thing in the world from her mind when Sean had taken her into his arms and kissed her. It had been only the two of them merging . . . soaring . . . loving, just as they had—

No, Rita wasn't the reason she'd stopped him— stopped herself, really. She'd been forced to choose five years before, and she had. She couldn't go back and undo that choice.

Or could she?

"Melissa?"

"I can't go through it all again, Sean," she said with painful simplicity.

"That was five years ago. A lifetime, you called it the other day. Look, I don't want to go through it all again any more than you do. But I do want a second chance."

"What—what does that mean?"

He gave a humorless little chuckle. "How could I know? You've changed. I've changed. But there's still something between us, sweetheart. We both know it. We both feel it. Why don't we just concentrate on that and forget about the past?"

She could never forget about it. Yes, she *had* changed. But one thing remained unaltered. She was a dancer. Ballet was her life and her love.

"What about Rita?"

Something—could it possibly be amusement?—tugged at the corner of his mobile mouth. "I give you my word, Rita will understand."

She smoothed the fabric of her dress. Perhaps Rita would understand, but she was not at all certain she did. Yet, Sean was right. There *was* something between them. . . .

"If—if I have dinner with you—" she began.

"I promise the most intimate thing I'll suggest for the rest of the evening is that we share a bottle of wine." His eyes glinted with teasing mockery. "And if you want to be on the safe side, you can order everything with extra garlic."

"I might just do that."

They dined at a popular Italian restaurant in the East 50s. The decor was timelessly elegant but comfortable, without the determined air of chic that Melissa found distasteful in many pricey eating places.

Despite Sean's joking about her passion for pasta, she opted for a simple veal dish. The meat was meltingly tender and its creamy sauce was sparked by the vibrant

tang of fresh lemon. A delicious dish of spinach, lightly
sautéed in olive oil and perfumed with garlic, accompanied the entree.

They decided on zabaglione for dessert. Melissa savored the sweetness of the warm and winy froth with a
sigh of satisfaction. She felt relaxed and replete.

"I won't be able to get into any of my costumes if I
keep eating like this," she observed ruefully to Sean as
she shook her head to the waiter's polite offer of a second
helping.

"You'll just have to figure out a way to burn off the
extra calories," Sean replied, spooning up the last mouthful of his dessert. She was struck by his air of sophis-
tication and confidence. He made no effort to impress
with his athletic celebrity or his business success, but he
was very clearly at home in this expensive, stylish en-
vironment. He had a bred-in-the-bone masculine grace
that she had come to recognize as very rare.

She stirred her spoon around thoughtfully, a small
frown shadowing her delicate features as she reflected
on her own vulnerability to his special qualities. Melissa
didn't delude herself that she was unique in her appreciation of him, yet she wondered how many women knew
how thoroughly his strength was tempered with gentle-
ness. Yes, he was proud and pigheaded about some things,
but he was capable of remarkable sensitivity and tenderness. . . .

"Melissa?"

Ye gods, she was doing it again, drifting off into
another reverie about Sean Culhane! And *this* time he
was right there, close enough to touch. She was acting
like some lovesick . . .

"Sorry," she said. "I was—um—thinking—"

"About dancing?" There was an edge to the question.

For a fleeting moment she wondered how he would
react if she told him he was the subject of her reflections.

"Not . . . exactly," she temporized. "You know, I never

realized until I injured myself how dancing filled up my days. Having had to stop, I'm discovering all kinds of holes in my life. Poor Nijinsky doesn't know what to make of my being home so much. He thinks I'm trying to take over his turf." She smiled suddenly. "I never thanked you for suggesting that I work at the youth center, did I? I know it's been only two classes, but it's really wonderful! At first I was afraid I wouldn't be much help, but now I think I'm doing a pretty good job."

"More than pretty good, from what I've seen. Have you discovered any budding ballerinas?"

"Well, there is one teenage boy named Tonio Martinez who's got a lot of potential. He's too old to start studying ballet seriously, but he'd do well in modern or jazz."

"Tonio—the boy with the permanent glower?"

"You can hardly blame him," Melissa declared with feeling. "Apparently everybody he knows makes fun of him because of his interest in dance. He's even gotten into some fights about it. Poor Tonio. I think deep down inside he's afraid there might be something abnormal about him." She played with the fragile stem of her crystal wineglass for a moment, then slanted a mischievous look across the table at Sean. "It's too bad I can't get you to take up ballet."

"I beg your pardon?"

"The sight of you in a pair of tights would convince Tonio—and everybody else—that there's nothing sissy about dancing."

"I'll bet."

"It was just a thought," she assured him innocently.

"She thinks too much. Such women are dangerous," he paraphrased.

"Julius Caesar," she replied. She'd taken a course in Shakespeare at N.Y.U. "And I seriously doubt that I have a 'lean and hungry look' after this dinner."

He grinned, acknowledging her quip with a nod of his head. "How's the coaching going?"

"All right so far," she answered, a bit surprised he mentioned it. "Dianne Kelso's very good. I think she's going to have a success with *AfterImages.*"

"She'll have to go some to match yours," he stated quietly, then recited unemotionally: "'In *AfterImages,* choreographer Bruno Franchiese has created another work of genius. In Melissa Stewart, he has discovered an exquisite instrument for the translation of that genius.'"

The shock of the words left her momentarily speechless. Those were the opening sentences of a rave review one of the world's most influential dance critics had written after the premiere performance of *AfterImages.* The praise had thrilled her mother yet left Melissa oddly unmoved.

"I had no idea—" she began.

"I was curious."

"Have you . . . have you ever seen *AfterImages?*"

"No. I was never quite that—curious."

"Oh." The slight hesitation before the final word struck her as peculiar, yet instinct warned her against pursuing the subject. She knew all too well that this turn of conversation could destroy the harmony that had flourished between them during their meal. She didn't want that.

Sean apparently felt the same way, because he deftly but determinedly changed the subject and began to tell her about his travels during the past week. A short time later he called for the check.

Their conversation was carefully casual during the taxi ride back to Melissa's apartment. In the back of her mind she began debating the wisdom of inviting him in. Although they had lingered over their dinner, it was still comparatively early, and she didn't want the evening to end. At the same time she was wary about how he might interpret an invitation to come upstairs again.

Sean took the matter out of her hands.

"I don't think I'll run the risk of your attack cat again," he said lightly. "Unless you want an escort inside?"

"Oh—no. That's not necessary," she assured him, uncertain whether she was relieved or disappointed. "I—dinner was lovely, Sean. Thank you. I'm very glad I went."

"My pleasure." He smiled warmly, the dimple at the corner of his mouth creasing deeply. "Look, I've got tickets for the game on Sunday. Are you free?"

With Sean, there could be only one game.

"Who's New York playing?"

"Pittsburgh."

"What about the seats? Are they any good?" she asked teasingly. Knowing him, they were probably on the fifty-yard line.

"I could sneak you onto the bench if you want."

"No, thank you. The last thing I need is to be squashed by a herd of tacklers going out of bounds. I'll take the stands."

"Terrific. I'll pick you up around noon." He dropped a chaste kiss on her forehead and said good night.

Sunday was gorgeous. The sun was shining, the sky was a vivid, sapphire-clear blue, and the air had a crisp seasonal tang to it. On the drive out to the stadium Melissa asked Sean for news of his former teammates—at least the ones she'd met. This triggered off a hilarious series of stories about locker-room antics and off-field hell-raising.

"He actually glued their cleats to the floor?" she asked in laughing disbelief as Sean held the door of his low-slung sports car open for her with a flourish.

"You've got it. And to make things worse, he used that quick-drying super-epoxy stuff. I think they ended up using a blowtorch to get the shoes free. Still, that's the kind of prank that's made New York famous."

"Yea, team!" she cheered.

He shut the car door and locked it. "Speaking of the team . . . I figured at the very least you'd wear the right colors today. Not that you don't look absolutely great, Twinkletoes—but black and blue?"

Melissa glanced down at herself, enjoying the compliment. She *felt* great at the moment—sparkling with laughter. She was wearing snug-fitting black cord jeans, boots, a black silk shirt, and a peacock-blue cable knit pullover. Her hair was stylishly done up in French plaits.

"Sorry," she apologized. "I'll make up for my faux pas by cheering extra loudly. Now, New York is the team with the big bird on its helmets, right?" she questioned, assuming a wide-eyed air of total ignorance.

"Sure, they are. And if they play real well, maybe they'll end up in the World Series," he mocked.

She sniffed disdainfully. "In any case, you're a fine one to criticize the way I'm dressed. I was positive you'd drag one of your lucky game jerseys out of retirement. But, no." She sighed dolefully.

Privately she thought Sean looked sensational in his jeans, a turtleneck, and a tweed jacket with suede patches on the elbows. His mirrored sunglasses were shoved back up on top of his head, and the mild September breeze was ruffling his hair.

"Well, actually—" He draped an arm around her shoulder, drawing her close so he could murmur into her ear. "I do have my jersey on underneath. I may look like a mild-mannered sports fan to you, but in reality—"

"You're Super Jock?" she suggested. "And when New York is trailing in the final moments of the fourth quarter, you suddenly rip off your clothes and—"

"Sean's going to rip off his clothes? I'd rather see that than a football game any day!"

"Rita!" Melissa turned, her mouth dropping open.

"Hi," Rita returned cheerfully. "Sorry we're late."

She was accompanied by a handsome, lithely built Latin-looking man in his early thirties.

"*Amigo,* long time no see." He greeted Sean with a flashing grin. The two men shook hands. Melissa stared back and forth between them and Rita, a delicate wrinkle of bewilderment creasing her forehead.

"Melissa, I want you to meet my husband, Miguel," Rita said. "Miguel, Melissa Stewart."

Miguel's dark eyes ran over her in friendly but frankly curious assessment. "Finally! I'm very pleased to meet you."

"I'm pleased to meet you, too," Melissa replied, wondering what he meant by the "finally." She hoped her face wasn't betraying her surprise. Rita was *married?* And her husband and Sean were good friends? "I—ah— I didn't realize you were married," she said to Rita.

"Nearly three years," Rita replied, linking her arm through Miguel's with a smile. "All thanks to Sean."

"Sean?"

"He introduced us," Miguel explained. "Something that earned him a permanent spot in my mama's heart. She was terrified I'd fall in love with some *gringa.*" He shot a mock-threatening look at Sean. "I, on the other hand, have spent the past few years plotting how to avenge myself on him."

Rita jabbed him in the ribs. Melissa sensed this was a regular routine with them. "What about me, *querido?* Sean promised me a handsome lawyer. Instead, I wound up with a skinny public defender!"

"With the way you cook, *chica,* I'll be skinny all my life. And I'm not a public defender now. I've moved up in the world."

"But your clientele hasn't improved."

"What do you do?" Melissa asked. The affection beneath their raillery was plain.

"I'm part of the city's gang-intervention program. Who better than a former gang member? Incidentally I hear we have an acquaintance in common. Tonio Martinez?"

"Tonio's in a gang?" she asked, shocked.

"By some miracle, no. But his two older brothers are, and I've had some dealings with them."

"Oh." Melissa's relief was visible. "Tonio has a lot of talent, you know. I'd like to figure out a way to get him some formal training. *And* reassure him there's nothing unmasculine about dancing."

"Peer pressure," Miguel said knowingly. "To tell the truth, I think Tonio's shown real guts sticking with the dancing this long."

"Well, I'm going to come up with something for him," Melissa vowed. She felt an instant liking for Miguel Perez; he was tough but caring. After a moment her determined expression took on a hint of mischief. "As a matter of fact, the other night I talked to Sean about the possibility of his putting on some tights—"

The Perezes laughed appreciatively at the suggestion.

"Forget about ripping your clothes off, Sean," Rita jibed. "I want to see you in tights."

"Dream on, Rita," Sean tossed back with an easy grin. He slipped his arm around Melissa's waist. "Why don't we go claim our seats?"

Because of the crowd's pushing into the stadium, the two couples got separated on the way in.

"Don't worry," Sean said as they maneuvered through the throng. "Our seats are all together."

"Oh." Melissa suddenly recalled Rita saying something to Sean about their being "on" for the weekend. Could she have been talking about coming to this football game?

"You looked a little stunned back there."

"I didn't expect to see Rita," she replied bluntly. "Why didn't you say something?"

"Rita and Miguel weren't absolutely sure they were going to be able to make it. I didn't want you to be disappointed."

Instead you let me end up standing there with my mouth hanging open, Melissa thought.

"You at least could have told me Rita was married!" She gave him a sharp, slightly accusatory look. "Especially Thursday night at my apartment. You know what I thought."

"Past tense? You don't think that anymore?"

"Of course not. Who could, after seeing Rita and Miguel together?"

"That's basically why I didn't tell you. I thought you'd be more likely to believe it if you saw for yourself."

"They do seem made for each other."

"My only successful effort at matchmaking."

"You like Rita a lot, don't you?" she asked suddenly. She couldn't totally shake her jealousy of the other woman. She'd really known Sean only for a few months. While they'd shared a passionate intimacy, Melissa still sadly felt they'd lacked a basic understanding of each other. Sean and Rita, on the other hand, had obviously been good and close friends for a number of years. Melissa envied that.

"Yes, I do," he replied simply. His green-gold eyes glanced shrewdly down at her. "To be honest, we came close to having an affair at one point. Luckily both of us were smart enough to realize that kind of involvement would have been a major mistake. So, instead of becoming lovers, we ended up being friends."

Melissa said nothing. She wondered if, looking back, Sean considered *his* involvement with her a major mistake. It was not a pleasant idea to contemplate.

Fortunately the game was exciting enough to keep Melissa's mind off such troubling thoughts. Miguel and Sean were knowledgeable and vocal New York fans, as were most of the people sitting around them. Predictably Sean was recognized and subjected to a great deal of attention. He handled it with low-key charm, managing to brush off interruptions without giving offense. He grinned at the repeated complaints that his old team hadn't been the same since his retirement.

After a shaky first half, New York surged back to win the game with a field goal in the final seconds of the fourth quarter. Melissa, Sean, Miguel, and Rita jumped to their feet, cheering lustily as time ran out. It was at that point that Melissa was forced to admit to herself that attending an outdoor football game—and behaving like a cheerleading jack-in-the-box—probably was not on Dr. David Goldberg's list of approved activities for injured ballerinas any more than pirouettes were.

Biting her lip, she managed to hold back a gasp of pain. She could do nothing to prevent the color from draining out of her cheeks.

"Melissa?" Sean said sharply, leaning toward her. "What's the matter?"

"Nothing," she said quickly, trying to smile.

"It's your knee, isn't it?"

"It—it's a little stiff, that's all." Bracing herself against the hurt, she flexed the joint carefully.

"Damn!" The anger in Sean's voice told her the stoic routine was not very convincing. "Sitting on cold concrete and hopping up and down for the past two hours— I should have thought about this. I'm sorry, sweetheart."

"What's wrong?" Miguel asked, noting Sean's concerned expression.

"Melissa's knee is acting up. It's my fault."

"Maybe you should sit down, Melissa," Rita suggested sympathetically. "You look awfully pale."

"I'm all right," Melissa insisted. "The joint's just tightened up a bit. I can work it out. Once I walk a little—Sean!" Her voice rose as she found herself swung effortlessly up into Sean's arms. "For heaven's sake, put me down!"

He shook his head, shifting her slightly so she was resting close against his chest.

"Sean!" Melissa protested, acutely aware that Rita and Miguel were grinning at them and that Sean's action had drawn some interested looks from the fans, who were now trying to leave the stands. "I'm all right, really."

"Humor me, Twinkletoes."

Recognizing that arguing wasn't going to get her anywhere—especially not back on her feet—Melissa brought
her arms up and linked them around his neck for stability.
"You can't carry me all the way back to the car," she
said.

"Can't I? Melissa, I used to wear equipment that weighs
more than you do. Just relax and enjoy the ride."

There *was* something infinitely comfortable about being
cradled with such gentle strength, yet the sensation of
her body against his was far from relaxing. She could
feel the tension in the well-conditioned muscles of his
arms, shoulders, and back as he began to move. The
spicy scent of his aftershave filled her nostrils. Melissa
found herself fighting against a seductive urge to melt
completely into physical surrender.

Rita and Miguel kept up a stream of conversation as
they walked down the stadium steps and eventually filed
out into the parking lot. Secretly Melissa felt a sense of
relief that Sean had insisted on carrying her. Her knee
did hurt quite badly. While it was not as severe as the
agony she'd experienced two weekends before in her
dressing room, she suspected it would have had her limping long before she reached Sean's car under her own
power.

"You're still very white, *amiga mía,*" Rita commented once they'd reached the car. Sean carefully de-
posited Melissa inside.

"Yeah, she is," he agreed flatly. "I think we should
take a raincheck on dinner."

Melissa's protests over this were brushed aside and
after a flurry of farewells the Perezes took their leave.
Sean got into the car and buckled his seat belt, waiting
patiently for Melissa to do the same. He started the engine
and put the car into gear, then skillfully maneuvered his
way through the confusion of traffic.

"I am sorry," Melissa said finally, breaking the silence
between them.

"Don't be. I should have realized the kind of stress this would put on your knee. How badly does it hurt?"

"I've danced with parts of my body feeling worse."

He made a disapproving sound. "Sure. You've danced with shin splints, tendonitis, stress fractures—"

"Sean, please." They'd disagreed about this many times five years before. Sean just could not fully comprehend the dancer's urge—compulsive need—to dance. Athletes drove themselves, too, of course, but dancers somehow saw themselves as serving on a higher, more demanding plane in the name of Art.

"Okay." The dimple creased at the corner of his mouth as though he were inwardly mocking his protectiveness. "Do you think you should call Dave Goldberg?"

"On a Sunday? Of course not!"

"What are you going to do about your knee then?"

She shrugged. "Probably go home, take two aspirin, and soak in a hot tub. If I put the heating pad on it tonight, it will be fine in the morning."

"How would some time in a Jacuzzi strike you?" Sean guided his car in and out of the traffic with expert skill, handling the sleek, powerful vehicle as though it were a natural extension of his body.

Melissa sighed wistfully, her eyes irresistibly drawn to the way his strong fingers gripped the steering wheel. His hands were beautifully shaped, with tanned skin and only a slight dusting of fine golden hair. Sportwriters had always praised his "quick" hands. Melissa had learned how slowly sensual . . . how erotically gentle . . . they could be.

"Melissa?"

She shook her head, clearing the fantasy. "Sorry. A Jacuzzi would be heavenly. But where do we find one?"

He glanced away from the road for a moment, his green-gold eyes teasing as they met her gray ones. "It just so happens I know a place with a private whirlpool."

"You do?" A peculiar shiver of anticipation ran up her spine as a questioning smile curved his lips.

"My apartment."

"But your apartment doesn't have—"

"My old apartment didn't have a Jacuzzi. I moved about two years ago. Bought a co-op near Central Park. I had a Jacuzzi and a few pieces of athletic equipment put in. My house is your house, as the cliché goes."

"Hmmm..." Melissa hesitated, suddenly uncertain. The idea of a Jacuzzi was very tempting, but the notion of being alone with Sean in his apartment...

He divined her thoughts with uncanny perception. "I'm not trying to lure you up to my place in order to ravish you, Twinkletoes. Nothing will happen that you don't want to happen."

Melissa almost laughed. Although she would never admit it to him, she was more concerned about handling her wants than his. Despite his aggressively seductive behavior in her apartment on Thursday, she knew Sean would not take something that was given unwillingly. But just how unwilling would she be?

She touched the tip of her tongue to her lips, moistening them as she shifted in the seat. "I—it would be very nice," she said slowly.

"Is that a yes?"

"I...suppose so." Her tone was still cautious.

"Melissa—"

"Yes. It's a yes."

CHAPTER FIVE

SEAN'S APARTMENT TOOK her by surprise. His previous one had been distinctly a bachelor's place. His new co-op, located in an exclusive and obviously expensive high-rise overlooking Central Park, had a much more solid and settled feel to it. The beige, cocoa-brown, and marine-blue color scheme had a distinctly masculine flavor, and there was a polished elegance to the decor.

The one indication of Sean's previous career as a sports star was a large, vividly colored original painting by LeRoy Neiman. This artist's vibrant technique had captured in time the portrait of a quarterback on the brink of passing a football.

"I—I like your apartment," Melissa said after looking around curiously.

He smiled, shucking off his jacket and dropping it casually on the back of a chair. She could see the smooth ripple of muscles under his snug-fitting turtleneck. He ran a hand carelessly through his hair. "Thanks. It's been a good investment. And I needed a bigger place for business entertaining."

"Oh." She nodded. There was a brief, awkward pause. *This was a mistake,* Melissa thought. *I never should have come up here with him.* "You—you mentioned a Jacuzzi?" she prompted.

He gave a small chuckle. She might feel as though she were treading on eggshells, but he seemed perfectly at ease. "Of course. Come on. And don't be alarmed—the whirlpool's in the master bath, which just happens to be off my bedroom."

His bedroom was on the same generous scale as the rest of the apartment. Done in various shades of beige, brown, and rust, it was dominated by an enormous bed. Melissa's eyes flickered over it nervously. How many women—?

There was an alcove off the bedroom that a woman might have used as a dressing room. Sean had equipped it for at-home workouts. There was a gleaming set of weights, a pulley apparatus for strengthening the upper body, a stationary bicycle, and a padded massage table. Adjoining this area was the master bathroom.

He flipped on the light. "Let me get you some towels," he said in a conversational manner. "Then I'll show you how to work the whirlpool."

"Th-thank you." While Sean had always practiced the physical and mental disciplines required of a top-flight athlete, Melissa had learned that he also had a sybaritic streak in his nature. That side of him was clearly evident in the azure, white, and silver luxury of the bathroom.

The walls were covered with mirrored tiles, the floor thickly carpeted in dark blue. There was a glassed-in shower in one corner. The sunken tub was large enough to accommodate at least two people.

Sean opened a built-in linen closet and extracted a

stack of fluffy blue towels. "Here you go," he said. "Now, about the tub—"

"It's practically big enough to drown in," Melissa remarked, laughing a little.

"Well . . . if you feel the need for a lifeguard—" His tawny brows went up as he made the offer.

"No, I don't think so," she replied breathlessly, averting her eyes for a moment as she flashed back on something. Shortly before their relationship had ended Sean had coaxed her into spending an entire night with him. Until then she'd always gotten up and returned home to the apartment she shared with her mother.

Sleeping—and waking up—in Sean's arms had been a uniquely pleasurable experience for her. Yet, in an odd way, the most intimate part of their time together had come when they'd both used the same bathroom. It had been unexplored territory for Melissa . . . a heady taste of what living with a man would be like.

Flushing slightly at the memory, she tried to turn her attention to Sean's explanation of how to use the whirlpool.

"Just watch the temperature," he warned her, turning on the faucets full blast. "It runs very hot. A tender-skinned little thing like you could get parboiled."

"I'll be careful," she promised.

"Do you want something to read while you soak? Or maybe a rubber duck to play with?"

She laughed. It was a rippling, silvery sound. "You have a rubber duck?"

"Well, no. But if you squeeze me in the right place, I have been known to go *quack*—"

Melissa shook her head. "I think I'll pass on that, thank you very much. I'll just relax and do nothing."

"Okay, Twinkletoes. Call if you need anything."

"I will."

Melissa undressed with graceful efficiency after Sean

left. She hung her clothing neatly on a hook on the back of the door, then tested the water in the tub with one toe. Satisfied, she turned off the faucets and slowly lowered herself in. The steaming water lapped gently up to the level of her pink-tipped breasts. With a blissful sigh she reached over and switched on the whirlpool.

The subtle massage of the churning, bubbling water and the muted hum of the whirlpool machinery exerted an almost hypnotic effect over her. The dull throb in her knee and the tension in her right leg eased. As her mind drifted off into an aimless labyrinth of daydreams, her lashes fluttered down. . . .

"You were wrong, sweetheart, you do need a lifeguard."

Melissa's eyes flew open and she stiffened, her pulse speeding up dramatically as she realized that Sean Culhane was standing by the sunken tub. He was clad only in his jeans.

Melissa had seldom felt more vulnerable. "Sean!" she exclaimed. Bringing her arms up, she crossed them protectively in front of her. At least the roiling water offered some shield against his scrutiny.

Even that concession to modesty was denied her a moment later when Sean very calmly leaned across her to switch off the Jacuzzi.

"Just what do you think you're doing?" she demanded.

"You've been in here nearly an hour, Melissa. Fifty-four minutes to be precise. When I suggested you take a Jacuzzi, I didn't intend for you to take up residence in here. I also damn well didn't intend for you to fall asleep!"

"I wasn't asleep!" she countered defensively.

"From where I was standing, you certainly didn't look awake."

The implications of this remark took a second to sink in. When they did, Melissa gasped in embarrassed outrage. Her cheeks, already faintly rosy from the heat of the bath, went an even deeper shade of pink.

"You've been watching—how long—?" she sputtered.

"Long enough," Sean replied mildly. "I *did* knock.
You didn't answer. I was afraid something might have
happened to you."

"I'm just fine, thank you!"

"Oh, I can see that. In fact, I'd say you were a lot
better than fine." His voice took on a teasing huskiness,
turning the words into a verbal caress.

Melissa swallowed hard. "I—I'd like to get out now,
Sean," she said after a few moments, striving to keep
her tone polite.

"Good idea," he agreed, picking up a large, luxuri-
ously napped towel from the counter and shaking it open.

"I'd also like you to leave."

"Hot water is debilitating. You may not be completely
steady on your feet."

"Not be—"

"Come on, Melissa," he continued firmly. "You won't
show me anything I haven't seen before. Besides, with
your knee—"

"I'm not helpless!"

"I never said you were."

There was a long pause. Then with all the poise she
could summon, Melissa rose slowly out of the tub. The
water sluiced down over the curves and hollows of her
slender body as she did so, lending a sheen to her fair
skin. For one horrible second she felt her knees go wob-
bly, but she stiffened them and her spine, forcing herself
to stand with unmoving dignity.

Strangely Sean's suddenly narrowed gaze did not stray
from her face. Wordlessly he handed her the bath towel.

She wrapped it around herself, giving silent thanks
that her fingers were steady. Stepping out of the tub, she
confronted him.

That was a mistake. Their eyes met and locked. What
she read so clearly in the molten depths of his made her

breath stop at the top of her throat. Her own eyes began to cloud.

With almost ritual deliberation his hands slid up her arms and over her smooth, naked shoulders before gently encircling the slim column of her throat. His thumbs stroked lightly at the hollow above the joining of her collarbone.

Her water-warmed skin was very sensitive. The barest brush of contact sent a quiver through her, racing along the network of nerve endings.

He bent his head and touched his lips to hers, teasing, tasting, relishing, with the thoughtful restraint of a gourmet savoring an unusual delicacy. With a small moan she yielded her mouth to him. He took only a brief, darting advantage before pulling back.

Melissa's lids fluttered open. Her huge gray eyes had gone smoky with emotion. "You promised—" she whispered. "You said nothing would happen."

He'd shifted his hands slightly. His thumbs were now tracing languid circles on the upper swell of her breasts. She could feel her nipples begin to tauten against the plush fabric of the towel.

"I said nothing would happen that you didn't want to happen," he corrected her softly. "And I think you want this as much as I do, Melissa." He kissed the soft curve where her neck met her shoulder. "Don't you?"

"Sean—"

His mouth found the same spot on the opposite side and she shuddered as she felt the nibble of his teeth against her flesh. "Don't you?" he repeated.

She did want it . . . him. For five long years she'd lived and loved through her dancing. Now her body—her soul—craved more.

But how much more? And how much would it cost in the end?

"Don't be afraid," he murmured, his lips moving up the line of her neck, finding the throbbing pulse point in the dainty hollow by her ear. He nipped the lobe. "I won't ask anything of you you don't want to give. Just let me love you."

And let me love you, a tiny voice inside her begged.

Slowly she slid her hands up his back, her fingers tracing the indentation of his spine. His skin was warm and smooth. She could feel his muscles moving, responding to her touch.

He sought and found her mouth once again, possessing it this time with a deeper, more demanding hunger. She met his appetite with a sudden yearning of her own, arching up and against him, feeling the virile thrust of his need and signaling hers.

Sean scooped her up into his arms and carried her out of the bathroom and to his bed. Night had fallen outside and none of the lamps in the room were on, yet she could see his strongly molded features quite clearly. Her awareness of him as she lay there, quivering with restless anticipation, was complete.

Placing one knee on the bed, Sean leaned over her, his expression very intent, his sensual mouth set in a controlled line. With one finger he traced a burning route from her lips, down her throat, to the barely revealed cleft between her breasts. Then, without hurrying, he slipped the finger under the towel that still covered her, and tugged. A moment later she was naked to the lingering exploration of his eyes . . . his hands . . . his mouth. . . .

She thought she heard him catch his breath. Hunger, hot and unashamed, flamed in the darkening depths of his green-gold gaze. An answering fire sparked to life inside her.

Melissa made an inarticulate sound of protest as he straightened suddenly.

"I'm not leaving you," he said softly. "I just don't want any barriers between us. Not now, love."

He unzipped his jeans and stripped them off without even a hint of self-consciousness. Discarding the garment on the floor in an impatient gesture, he stood for a moment, surveying her pliant, supine body. In the dim, shadowed room her fair skin had taken on a pearly, almost magical luster.

Boldly Melissa let her eyes rove over his superb male nudity, feasting on the elegant strength of his long legs and well-muscled thighs . . . the hair-rough, breadth of his powerful chest . . . and the classic molding of his shoulders. He made no effort to hide the sure sign of his arousal.

There was invitation in the way she studied him and in the way her lips pouted then parted for his kisses. She lifted one arm to him, beckoning.

"You want this to happen, don't you?" he asked.

She nodded, her hand still reaching out for him.

"Say it."

"I . . . want this. . . . I want you."

The mattress gave slightly as he joined her on the bed, stretching out beside her. He took the hand she had extended to him and kissed it.

Five years before, Sean had made love to her and taught her, with soaring tenderness, the physical truths the pas de deux she danced only palely imitated. Now, as he pulled her to him, she experienced once again the exultant harmony two finely trained and instinctively attuned bodies could make.

At first he was more choreographer than partner—he set the pace, designed the movements, molded her to his inner vision of perfect passion. Their mouths met and fused in a long, searching kiss. Melissa gave herself up to the embrace with a breathless ardor, reveling in the feel of his hard lips and plundering tongue.

Sean broke the kiss at last, his mouth trailing a searing path down to her breasts. He captured one nipple with his lips, sucking until the rosy peak was taut. He slowly nibbled his way across the delicate swell of her bosom to her other breast, favoring it with the same arousing homage.

Her arms had come up, locking around his neck. She gasped suddenly, arching as he insinuated one hand between her thighs to stroke the silken inner skin then search out the sensitive secrets of her femininity.

"Sean! Please!" Her bones were melting. Her bloodstream was filled with fiery champagne—all heat and bubbles. She wanted him...needed him...now!

He touched again knowingly. "I've been waiting five years for this," he murmured thickly. "I want to wait just a little more...make it last."

Pleasure prolonged can become torture, just as desire too long denied can fester in frustration. At that moment, a small moan breaking from her lips, Melissa began to meet and match her partner, her lover. She moved her body sinuously against his, savoring the heated erotic contrast between his hard strength and her yielding softness. Daintily she nipped at the cord of his neck, then nuzzled her mouth yearningly against the tawny mat of his chest hair, her tongue seeking the tight circles of his nipples.

"Meli—God!" His shuddering response to her teasing touch set off a thrilling rush of pleasure within her. She gloried in the feel of it.

There was no sound in the room but the counterpointed rhythm of their shallow, rapid breathing and the throaty whispers of softly voiced endearments. Yet, inside each of them a symphony was swelling—the same symphony. They could both hear it. Surrendering to the force of it, they began to move.

Finally, when she felt her heart would burst or her body explode into flames, Sean moved up and over her. Melissa welcomed him, giving and receiving as their passion built to its final crescendo. She was flying, lighter than air, locked in the arms of her perfect partner.

Release came for both of them in the same rapturous split-second. Sean captured her mouth like a starving man when that moment arrived, so her moaning invocation of his name was lost beneath the devouring exploration of his lips.

There was silence afterward. The ecstasy they had experienced together had driven out the need for words. The intimate intertwining of legs and arms, the languid brush of lips over perspiration-slick skin, the smoky exchange of glances—they made mere speech unnecessary.

Finally Sean shifted himself away from her. As his weight eased off her body, Melissa felt an aching emptiness. She wanted to go on holding him, clinging to him.

"I'd throw roses at you and scream brava," Sean declared unsteadily. "But I don't think I have the strength."

She had not expected protestations of love. She was not certain what she had expected. In a strange way this teasing yet tender comment seemed to be precisely what she wanted—needed—to hear.

Melissa began to laugh. It was a voluptuous, not girlish sound, bubbling up from her very core. "A-at least you must have enough reserves to t-take your curtain call," she returned.

Sean managed a crooked grin and chuckled. "Give me a few minutes, and I'll work up the energy for an encore." He turned onto his side, facing her. She saw the smooth ripple of finely trained muscle beneath his skin as the sheet fell away from his torso. A tremble ran through her as he traced a caressing trail up the silken line of her thigh and hip.

She snuggled against him, pressing her mouth gently against the crisp mat of his chest hair. Her own fingers moved delicately to rediscover the sleek power of his lean body. Breathing in deeply, she blissfully inhaled his musky, masculine scent.

"Melissa—"

"Mmm?"

"I know it's a little late to ask, but did you come prepared for this?"

"Prepared?" she repeated blankly.

He pulled away from her slightly, his eyes narrowing. "Precautions. Birth control."

Her heart missed a beat. Oh, God, she'd never even considered—

She did some rapid mental calculations. She'd gone on the pill during her affair with Sean—her mother had seen to that after a lacerating and acid-tongued lecture— but she'd stopped taking it immediately after the break-up.

"Melissa?"

She peered up at him through a veil of dark lashes. "There's no problem," she said honestly. "It's not the time of the month for—I'm not going to get pregnant."

"No, I don't suppose you are," he observed flatly, rolling onto his back and staring up at the ceiling. "Just for the record, though, not all men walk away from their responsibilities."

Her lips tightened as she realized what he was talking about. "You mean not all men are like my father," she said quietly. "I know that."

There was a long pause. She sat up, wrapping the sheet around her.

"Do you ever wonder about him?"

She closed her eyes. Why, *why* had she told him the truth? She had never shared it with anyone else, had never even come close to it.

"I used to when I was little," she answered. "When I thought he was dead. Then my mother told me how he'd left her and I decided it didn't really matter. At least Mama wanted me. She gave up so much."

And she never let you forget it, a tiny voice whispered. *So you had to become the dancer she couldn't be. You studied, sweated, worked, and hurt . . . and when it finally came time for the bows and bouquets, wasn't it her triumph more than yours?*

"What kind of dancer was your mother?"

"A good one," she said automatically. In truth, she had no idea. She'd never seen her mother dance. The only proof she had of her mother's "career" was a wrinkled and yellowing program from a long-forgotten and unsuccessful Broadway show. The name "Verna Stewart" was next to the last in the chorus listing. She took a deep breath. "Sean, I don't want to talk about this."

He sat up beside her. Steeling herself, she met his searching gaze steadily. "Why not?"

"Because if we talk about it, eventually we're going to fight. And I don't want to do that. Not now, please."

She had no idea how vulnerable she seemed at that moment. The crystalline appeal in her eyes revealed very clearly how easily she could be shattered. True, she was stronger and more confident of herself than she had been five years before; but the self-awareness that time and success had given her had also opened her eyes to some truths she had not yet fully accepted.

For a moment Sean seemed on the verge of pushing her, but he backed off. "What do you want?"

She swallowed, brushing back the stray tendrils of dark hair that had come loose and curled silkily over her smooth, alabaster-pale forehead. "I want you to hold me," she said. "And I want us to make love again. Like before."

But it was not as it was before when he reached for her. This time the urgency was on her side . . . the desperate desire to prolong every kiss, every caress, to the brink of madness was hers. Yet when he finally took her, it was with a raging tenderness and a driving passion that seemed to shudder out of the depths of his soul.

* * *

"You know," he murmured afterward, his fingers stroking slowly up and down her back as she lay curved against him, "the first time I made love to you five years ago, I was terrified I'd hurt you."

"You were afraid?" she asked, wondering. As she remembered it, he'd been commandingly, confidently gentle, soothing her instinctive fears and initiating her with arousing expertise. She had been shyly eager to please, but awkwardly conscious of her inexperience.

"Not just because you were a virgin," he went on. "But when I undressed you, Melissa, I thought you were the most exquisite woman I'd ever seen, all ivory innocence. I felt like the Incredible Hulk next to you. God, I was shaking like a clumsy teenager."

"Never," she assured him, brushing her lips along the determined line of his jaw, savoring the salty tang of his perspiration. "As for being the Incredible Hulk—I always pictured you as Superman." Her eyes went misty with remembered pleasures. "You didn't hurt me, Sean. It was wonderful."

"You're wonderful."

"We both are." She smiled at him, a radiant and hopeful expression. The storm had been averted—for now.

Eventually, reluctantly, Sean got up. He donned his jeans again, then tugged on a faded University of Pennsylvania sweatshirt. Grinning at her boyishly, he searched through his closet and finally tossed her a dark-blue velour robe.

"Try this for size," he instructed.

"Why?" she asked, lifting her brows. She was sitting up, the bed linen rucked around her, unbraiding her hair. The damp heat of the whirlpool had made it wave.

"Have you ever heard of dressing for dinner?"

"Oh. Are you hungry?" She eased herself lightly off the bed and pulled on the robe. It was far too large for her and showed an alarming tendency toward gaping immodestly in front. She wrapped the garment as snugly as she could, and knotted the belt tightly about her slender waist.

"Yes. I'm hungry for food at the moment. I might work up an appetite for something else afterward."

"Really?" Her eyes sparkled provocatively as she combed her fingers through her hair. "Well, you know what a picky eater I am. I hope I'll like what's on the menu. Both now . . . and afterward."

"I believe Madame will enjoy the speciality of the house."

She pretended to ponder the idea. "That depends. Is it fresh?" Her expression was innocently angelic.

"Absolutely," Sean replied, giving her a quick swat on the bottom. "And so are you, Twinkletoes. Into the kitchen. Let's see what we can cook up."

They made omelettes. Sean did most of the actual cooking; Melissa was assigned duties as chief scullery maid. They dined casually in the cheerfully decorated breakfast alcove in the kitchen, chatting companionably, bantering jokingly, and exchanging tidbits of food and sips of wine.

Once their plates were rinsed and placed in the dishwasher, they adjourned to the living room. The soft semi-classical strains of a popular motion picture soundtrack filled the room as Sean switched on his stereo.

Melissa sat down in the corner of one of the room's modular sofa units, curling her feet up under her. She made another adjustment of the robe as she leaned back, enjoying the music and savoring the last mouthfuls of the dry but slightly fruity white wine they'd drunk with dinner.

"Dinner was delicious," she complimented Sean after he crossed back from the stereo and sat down near her. He stretched his legs out in front of him with a quiet sigh of relaxed satisfaction.

"Thanks. Your assistance was invaluable." He smiled

as he lifted his wineglass to her.

"Na zdrovie," she said, returning the toast. She finished the last drops of wine and put her glass down on a smoked glass and metal end table by the sofa.

"Russian?" Sean drained his glass in a quick swallow. "Comrade Volnoy's influence, no doubt."

"I've picked up a few words here and there. But Yuri's made amazing progress with his English, considering he's been in the United States for only two years."

"From what I've read, he doesn't seem to have any problems communicating."

"Well, it wasn't exactly easy when he first came to the MBT after he defected. There was a lot of reliance on sign language in the beginning. Fortunately most dancers are good at pantomime. Plus, one ballet class tends to be like another, whether it's at the Kirov or in Kalamazoo."

"That wasn't the kind of communicating I meant."

Melissa gave him a puzzled look. There was a mocking quality to his comment. "I don't—" she began, then broke off as comprehension dawned. "Oh! *That* kind of communicating!" She laughed gaily, tossing her hair back. The front of the robe parted slightly with the movement, offering Sean a tantalizing glimpse of her breasts. "Yes, I suppose you have a point. Sex appeal has a language all its own, and Yuri definitely is fluent in it."

Sean's mobile mouth thinned and twisted at this, but he said nothing. There was an odd expression in his eyes as he watched her. She shifted, wondering what he was thinking.

"You still sit with your legs tucked up under you like a little girl," he observed at last.

Melissa made a face, adopting a more "adult" posture. There was a discreet flash of thigh as she did so. "It's a defense mechanism, to tell the truth. I'm trying to hide my feet."

"Hide your feet? That makes about as much sense as

a pro quarterback trying to disguise his throwing arm."

"I didn't claim it made sense. Most dancers have a love-hate relationship with their feet." She felt a quiver of trepidation as she said the word *dancers*. When it drew no noticeable reaction from Sean, she went on. "We depend on them for our livelihood, of course, but they seem so big and ugly."

"You call these big?" Sean questioned, leaning down with lightning swiftness and grabbing her ankles. Melissa let out an indignant squeal as he unbalanced her, shifting her body so her feet were resting in his lap.

"Sean! For heaven's sake!" She was acutely conscious that her highly arched feet carried more than their share of calluses and blisters. It was an occupational hazard.

"As for ugly . . ." He ran a finger experimentally along the sole of one of her imprisoned feet.

"D-don't!"

"Ah-ha! So the lady has big, ugly, *ticklish* feet." There was a devilish glint in his eyes.

"Sean! P-please—don't!" She experienced a deliciously dangerous sense of anticipation.

He quirked a brow. "Ve vill remember zees," he told her in an atrocious German accent. "It's a good thing you don't want to be Mata Hari, Melissa. The enemy wouldn't have to torture you for classified information. They could tickle it out of you."

"You're crazy, Sean Culhane!"

"So I have been told before."

"Will you give me back my feet, please?" She'd never thought of her feet as an erogenous zone before, but the warm, caressing possession of his hands around her heels and the gentle stroke of his thumbs on her ankles were sending tremors of excitement racing up her legs.

He shook his head calmly. "No, I'm becoming strangely attached to this portion of your lovely anatomy. Maybe I'm developing a foot fetish."

"Terrific." She was forced to redrape the robe again.

The gleam in Sean's eyes told her he'd already enjoyed a full visual inventory. "I'm being held captive by a kinky quarterback."

"Not kinky," he objected. "At least not yet. I have to work into this gradually. Let's see. Maybe I could start by collecting your cast-off pointe shoes."

"That's a wonderful idea," she laughed. "Considering I go through at least a dozen pairs a week, you shouldn't have any problems."

"I'll bronze them." He counted her toes with playfully exaggerated concentration. "Ten toes in satisfactory working order," he reported. After a moment he began massaging her feet, flexing them carefully, his strong fingers inscribing provocative designs on her flesh. Gradually he abandoned that part of her anatomy and started to knead her calves.

"How's your knee?" he asked, slipping his hand higher.

Melissa tilted her head back and expelled a shaky breath. Her gray eyes had gone smoky. She moistened her lips before speaking.

"W-wonderful," she breathed. She'd never known it was possible to be both relaxed and aroused. Her eyelids fluttered down as she let herself surrender to the compelling caress of his knowing hands.

"I must be losing my touch."

"I . . . don't . . . think so," she contradicted him, quivering as his fingers edged slowly, seductively, upward. His hand moved beneath the hem of the robe.

"I don't know," he remarked dubiously. "This is supposed to stimulate you, Melissa. You seem to be going to sleep."

Going to sleep?! He'd barely reached the top of her kneecaps and she was already a trembling blob of jelly. Her stomach was a mass of excited butterlfies and her breasts were peaking yearningly against the velvety fabric of the robe. She could feel the melting ache between her thighs. Imagining his hands stroking over the whole of her body, she shifted in a lithe, inviting movement that was an evocative combination of stretch and wriggle.

"I promise you, I'm not going to sleep, Sean."

"No?"

"I'm very much awake."

"Of course, if you did happen to doze off, we could perform that famous scene from *Sleeping Beauty*."

"Aaa, and what w-would that involve?"

"Oh, I'm sure you must remember," he said huskily. Dreamily Melissa let him pull her up and into his arms. She arched into the embrace fluidly. "The handsome prince awakens the beautiful sleeping princess with a kiss."

"And then?"

"And then . . . something . . . like . . . this."

CHAPTER SIX

SHE SPENT THE night with him, her soft, love-sated body curved intimately against his hard masculine form. It was the sensual slide of his palm leisurely exploring up the silken line of her leg and hip that roused her from her contented slumber.

"Good morning," Sean said softly as she shifted, looking up at him with a drowsy smile. He was leaning on one elbow, studying her. She had the feeling he'd been watching her for some time.

"Good morning," she returned, stretching slowly, relishing the sense of physical well-being that was blossoming within her like a flower under sunlight. Although the bedclothes were pulled modestly up around her shoulders, the sheet covered only the lower half of his body. Her gray eyes wandered over the strong lines of his sleekly muscled torso, marking how the tawny mat of chest hair arrowed down to his flat stomach and beyond.

Her mind's eye very pleasurably supplied the details of what the sheet hid.

Sean chuckled hoarsely and brushed his mouth over hers. She returned the kiss warmly, teasing her tongue insinuatingly over his lower lip.

"Melissa—" He broke the kiss, sitting up and running his hand casually through his thick hair. There was nothing casual about the gleam in his eyes.

"Yes?" After a moment she sat up next to him, not bothering to pull the bedclothes around her. The long tumble of her hair veiled her rose-tipped breasts like ebony silk.

"If Sleeping Beauty looked and behaved like you, I guarantee the prince wouldn't have stopped with a kiss."

"You don't think so?"

"No," he growled. "I don't."

"But I thought all princes were paragons of self-control," she observed with a small sigh. Keeping her expression carefully wistful, she very slyly moved one hand under the sheet and over toward Sean. "Then again, I don't recall your stopping with a kiss last night."

"I never claimed to be a prince. In fact—my God! *Melissa!*" Her name came out in a shocked groan. A moment later she found herself pressed flat on her back, her wrists pinioned against the pillow on either side of her head.

"Did I do something wrong?" Five years ago she'd been content to let Sean take the initiative in their lovemaking. Too uncertain and inexperienced to experiment, her only desire had been to please Sean as much as he pleased her. While the past five years hadn't added to her sexual experience, hours of listening to Laurette Fishkin's highly indiscreet confidences had increased her theoretical knowledge of male physiology. She only hoped her practical application of that knowledge hadn't been as ill-advised as Sean's reaction seemed to indicate.

"Sweetheart, in some places what you were about to

do is classed as an immoral practice. It's also likely to lead to your learning a few positions I don't think they teach in ballet class."

"I'm always interested in learning something new." He was leaning over her in such a way that he was using his weight rather than his superior strength to control her freedom of movement. It was a technique that was as arousing for the captive as it was for the captor.

"It could require a great deal of rehearsal," he warned, kissing each corner of her mouth.

"I'm ready." She arched with inviting grace.

"And you'll need a course of private lessons."

"Coaching, too?"

"Coaching, too." He lowered his head, his warm breath fanning over her shoulders and neck. Melissa wondered if he could feel the accelerated beat of her heart. She gasped in pleasure as his lips closed over one of her nipples, his tongue playing around it with tantalizing skill. Her hands clenched at the intensity of the sensation and she gasped again as he transferred his erotic attentions to the other taut peak.

"Sean—"

"You have to warm up for this sort of lesson." His voice was ragged. She felt the nudge of his knee between her legs and yielded to the pressure immediately.

"Wh-what about a m-mirror?"

"A mirror?"

"It, ahhh, helps if you can see what you're doing."

He pressed his mouth briefly to the fragrant cleft between her delicate breasts. "I can see what I'm doing just fine, love."

The effect of Sean's lovemaking, and her wanton response to it, lingered deliciously for many hours. It dulled her disappointment at hearing that business would be taking him out of the city for several days and cocooned her against the usual complement of everyday urban aggravations. Even a particularly rigorous physical therapy session did not straighten the alluringly preoccupied smile that curved her lips.

"Is not rehearsal that makes you smile so," a playfully reproving voice said into her ear late that afternoon. "Rehearsal is terrible. Should make you cry."

"Hmmm?" Melissa breathed dreamily, a soft flush mantling her cheeks. Her dark hair, worn loose and clipped off her face with a pair of combs, moved like a silken curtain as she turned her head. Abruptly she came back to reality. "Oh! Yuri! Hello."

One of the world's most acclaimed male dancers sat down on the floor of the rehearsal hall beside her, grinning boyishly. While Yuri Alexandrovich Volnoy was the epitome of elegance onstage, he was the ultimate gypsy urchin in class and rehearsal. His damp brown hair clung to his head in shaggy disarray, and there was a scampish sparkle in his wide-set brown eyes.

"Good to see you smile," he declared, stretching out his muscled legs and flexing his feet. "Even if my dancing is not the reason for it."

Melissa gathered her thoughts. "Well, actually, it *is* your dancing that brought me here. I'm hoping you'll do me a favor."

"Favor?" He picked up a towel and rubbed his head with it. "Strange you should say. There is favor you could do me, Melissa." He slung the towel around his neck and leaned forward. "You must become cured in your most beautiful leg, *dushka*."

"Soon, Yuri," she promised with a smile.

"If is not soon, I will be ruined. Your knee is hurt. My career is destroyed." He sighed tragically.

"Oh, really?" She was used to Yuri's flair for the melodramatic. It was part of his charm and one of the reasons he was such a successful performer.

"*Da*, really. The other night we were to dance *Swan Lake*, you and I."

"I know." Regret clouded her eyes.

"They give me Emilie in your place!" he said with a disgusted gesture. "One minute I am to have a delicate angel as partner, then I have this—this—lady giant!" He spat out a word that sounded like a Russian curse.

Melissa repressed a giggle. Emilie Devereaux was a marvelous dancer, but she had the misfortune of being five feet seven inches tall in her bare feet. This made her almost the same height as the compactly built Yuri. On pointe, she towered over him.

"Yuri, it can't have been that bad," she sympathized. "I know Emilie is difficult to partner—"

"Difficult? Impossible! Emilie as swan? Bah! She is two-ton canary. *And* she steps on my toe in pirouette!"

Now Melissa did laugh. Although Yuri's command of English was uncertain, he watched a great deal of television and had a knack for latching onto particularly descriptive turns of phrase.

Yuri glared at her in mock indignation. "Is fine for you to laugh, Melissa," he said in an injured tone.

"Well, you won't have to worry about Emilie this week, will you?" she soothed. "I see you're scheduled to dance with Stephanie tomorrow night. You can't say she's a two-ton canary."

"No. She is—how do you say?—all skinny and bones. Is like partnering dry stick." He grimaced distastefully.

"Yuri!"

He sniffed disdainfully. "I am man. I want feel of woman in my arms when I dance. Is one reason I am liking very much to partner you. Very feminine body." He smiled.

Melissa glanced down at herself. "Oh, come on," she protested. "I'm not exactly centerfold material."

He frowned. "What is that, please?"

She shaped the outline of a curvaceous figure.

He took a few moments to sort this out. "You are meaning naked women in magazines?" he inquired.

"Yes." She wished she hadn't brought it up.

"Is boring," he stated dismissively. "I look at them once, maybe twice. It does not turn on my engine. But to dance with you, that is very sexy. All other dancers say so."

"For heaven's sake!"

"You know Jean-Claude? The one who wants to be ballerina? Even he tells me if he can dance with you, he might start liking girls, not boys. Is fact. Is very beautiful, your body."

Melissa averted her eyes for a moment, both pleased and embarrassed. For a long time she'd felt very unhappy and uncomfortable with her body. In the ballet world, where willowy, sylphlike flatness was the accepted standard of perfection, her small but full breasts and delicately curved hips had caused her much professional anguish. Conversely outside the confines of the MBT—on a personal level—she'd always felt like a pale asexual shadow of a woman.

Until she'd met Sean Culhane. He'd made it plain he found her delectably female and extremely desirable. The first time they'd made love he'd undressed her with infinite slowness, voicing his appreciation, his adoration, in soft erotic whispers. There had been heated kisses and lingering, exploratory caresses, all of it washing away her self-doubts and insecurities in a tide of passion. She'd been utterly beautiful with him . . . and for him.

"You are smiling again," Yuri commented.

Melissa shook her head. "Sorry."

"Is no need. He must be very good lover."

"I—l-lover?" she managed to get out, feeling as though she'd been hit in the face with a bucket of ice water. *Laurette*, she thought. *Laurette Fishkin, I am going to kill you!*

"Ummm," he nodded, surveying her complacently. "Is obvious. You have a shine. That is word, *da? Nyet!* Glow! You have glow." He grinned proudly. "I have always known you must have lover somewhere. From the first time I partner you, is plain you do not dance like virgin."

"Are you—are you trying to say you can tell whether or not a woman is a virgin by the way she dances?" Melissa demanded in a shaky undertone.

He seemed surprised by her disbelief. "Of course. Is very nice to be virgin for *Sleeping Beauty* and maybe for beginning of *Giselle,* but to perform pas de deux with man, to have it be more than steps, ballerina has to be woman, not girl."

Melissa stared at him fixedly. "I suppose that's why you've been sleeping your way through the corps of every company that comes to town? For the sake of the dance?"

"I had not thought of that," he remarked contemplatively. Yuri made no secret of his Don Juan tendencies and, for the most part, he loved and left his various bedmates on the best of terms. "Maybe that is what I should say to very stubborn girl who tells me *nyet.*" He cocked his head, a mischievous gleam in his eyes. "Is good idea, you think?"

Melissa laughed. "I didn't know there were any stubborn girls in your life, Yuri Alexandrovich."

"Maybe one, maybe two," he admitted with a wink. After a moment his expression grew serious. "Are you ever wondering why I never come off to you?"

It took Melissa several seconds to figure out the change in subject—and Yuri's fractured phraseology. "What? Oh! You mean come *on* to me."

"That is the way to say it?"

"Yes. At least if you're talking about you and—and me—"

"Da. Is very confusing, this English. So many ways to say something so simple." He shrugged resignedly. "But you have wondered?"

"Well—" While she adored dancing with Yuri and could understand why so many women fell victim to his

Slavic charm, she was not personally attracted to him. At the same time, however, she'd felt a nagging sense of inadequacy over the fact that he'd never ever tried to flirt with her. "I suppose—I mean, you do seem to have worked your way through just about every other ballerina in town."

"Not so many as that," he protested mildly. "Would be exhausting. I tell you truth, Melissa. Are many women in world for making love. But only few for dancing. What I feel when I am onstage with you is very special. What we could do offstage, maybe would not be so special." There was an unexpected shrewdness in his eyes. "We have understanding when we dance. In making love . . . for me, is passing pleasure. For you, I think it must be more. Is not so?"

Slowly she nodded, thinking of Sean. She'd given herself to him for far deeper reasons than pleasure.

"You are smiling again."

"I know." It was as though the law of gravity had suddenly been reversed, pulling the corners of her lips irresistibly upward. They both laughed. It was the easy laughter of friends.

"Good," Yuri grinned. "You are not offended. Now you will tell me this favor you are wanting? Whatever it is, I, Yuri Alexandrovich Volnoy, am your slave. Unless you want me to dance again with Emilie. Then *I* am offended."

"It's nothing that awful," she assured him. She quickly explained about the class she was teaching at the youth center. Not realizing how intensely she was telling her story, she went on to describe Tonio Martinez and the problems he was facing.

"They are peasants, these children of yours?"

"Not peasants exactly," she returned, knowing that Yuri's understanding of the divisions in American society was hazy at best. "But they don't have much, Yuri. They're what some people call underprivileged."

"Peasants," he repeated firmly with none of his usual frivolity. "That I know about, *dushka*. When I was a young boy back in Soviet Union, I am not having many privileges either." He waved away the memory. "I will come and dance for you with pleasure. Is Thursday okay for doing? Tomorrow, with performance, would be hard."

"Thursday will be perfect."

"Then that is what it shall be."

She dropped a quick kiss on his cheek. "Thank you so much, Yuri."

"You are welcome." He got to his feet in a smooth movement. "Now, you stay for more rehearsal," he instructed. "Should be very funny."

It *was* funny, in an awful sort of way. For one reason or another the MBT was having an off day, and the rehearsal session degenerated into chaotic hilarity before the dance master finally gave up in a fit of disgust. Yet the smile Melissa wore as she drifted out of the theater had very little to do with the backstage comedy of errors she had witnessed.

Sean...his face, voice, touch...filled her mind. Was she falling in love with him all over again? Had she ever fallen *out* of love with him? The first day at the sports clinic, it had been as though a part of her soul had been encased in ice for five years and the mere sight of him had been enough to melt the frigid barrier. It had seemed so right, so inevitable.

He'd said with an emotion she still couldn't define that he was now willing to "settle" for what he could get. What did that mean? An affair?

And what would she "settle" for after all this time? She was honest enough to admit that she wanted Sean, needed him.

But she wanted—needed—to dance, too. Was there a way to find a balance? Could she be dancer *and* woman?

She was still mulling this over when she returned to

her apartment. Nijinsky, clearly irate about being left alone overnight, made his feline displeasure known by devoting himself to trying to trip her every time she moved.

"I think you're jealous, Nij," Melissa said finally, narrowly missing stepping on his tail as she opened the refrigerator. She removed a number of items. There was the requisite cat food for her pet, plus a can of tuna fish and a bottle of organic apple juice for herself.

Jealous. She clicked her tongue, recalling her initial feelings about Rita Perez. She had been jealous of her and of her obvious closeness to Sean. Having met Miguel, Melissa realized she'd misread the situation, yet she still felt a trace of envy toward the attractive social worker. And she felt more than a trace of envy toward all the women she knew Sean had been involved with during the past five years and might *still* be involved with.

After feeding Nijinsky she took her Spartan dinner into the living room. Juggling her plate and juice bottle, she switched on the evening news, then curled up in the corner of the couch.

The anchorman had just finished reporting on the latest from Wall Street when the telephone in the kitchen rang. Nijinsky, with diabolical positioning, managed to make her hurried dash to pick it up into an obstacle course.

"Are you trying to kill me?" she demanded as she finally reached the phone and snatched up the receiver.

"Is who trying to kill you?"

Melissa melted against the wall. "Sean!" she said delightedly, then yelped as Nijinsky began nibbling on her ankle. "Leave me alone!"

"Melissa, what's going on?" His voice was velvety with amusement. She could picture the flash of the dimple at the corner of his mouth.

"My cat is trying to do me in."

"Why?"

"I think Nijinsky's jealous because I left him alone last night."

"If that's the case, you're going to have problems. I don't think you're going to be spending many nights at home with him in the future."

"Nijinsky usually sleeps with me," she confided, her mouth curving into a pleased smile.

"That must make your love life interesting." The comment was made lightly, but Melissa could hear the question lurking behind it. Sean wasn't the type to impose a sexual double standard, but she sensed he disliked the idea that there might have been other men in her life. A small voice urged her to set his mind at rest, yet she held back. While she hadn't been able to hide the fact that he had been her first lover, she wasn't ready to tell him he'd been her only one as well.

"I haven't had any complaints."

"I see." The tone was on the disgruntled side of neutral. Could he be jealous, too?

"I'm so glad you called," she said, changing the subject. "I wasn't sure if you would."

"When I was over at your apartment the other day, I took the precaution of writing down the number on your telephone."

"Oh." Good, she thought.

"So, what are you doing now? Aside from saving yourself from your homicidal cat, I mean."

"Nothing much. What about you?"

"I'm missing you like hell."

"Me, too. Where—where are you exactly?"

"At my hotel. I'm getting dressed for that congressional roast I told you about."

"The one for the congressman who used to play pro football?"

"Right. I just hope I can hold on to my concentration long enough to get through my speech."

"You've never had any trouble concentrating."

"On you, sweetheart, no. That's part of the problem."

"Really?"

"Don't sound so innocent. I've been embarrassing myself all day because of you."

"What do you mean?"

"Well, for one thing, I had lunch with a friend of mine. He's a lawyer with the Justice Department's task force on organized crime involvement in professional sports. He wanted to bounce a few thoughts off me."

"And?"

"And about halfway through the meal he gave up. He said he couldn't discuss a serious subject with a man wearing what he described as a 'well-laid' look."

"He didn't!"

"Oh, I can assure you, he did."

"Well, if it makes you feel any better, I couldn't stop smiling all day. Yuri told me I had a glow."

"Volnoy? You went to the MBT today?"

"I needed to talk to Yuri about doing me a favor."

"Let me guess. He said yes to you."

"Eventually. I asked him to come up to the youth center and dance. If anybody can show Tonio that ballet isn't something sissy, it's Yuri."

"When's he due to appear?"

"Thursday. He's got a performance tomorrow." She twisted the phone cord around her finger. "When are you coming back?"

"Friday, I think. I've got a full calendar down here in D.C. tomorrow and then I go out to Chicago. If I hustle, I may be able to catch a plane and get back into town late Thursday night."

"Hustle, hustle," she urged.

"Honey, if my old head coach had sounded like you, New York would have had a permanent lock on the Super Bowl."

"It's all in the inflection."

"You've got terrific inflection."

"So do you."

There was a short pause. When Sean spoke again there was a definite thickness in his voice. "You wouldn't consider grabbing a shuttle from LaGuardia and coming down to Washington, would you?" he asked.

"Tonight?"

"Yeah."

"Well—"

He laughed suddenly. "On second thought, you'd better not. If I knew you were going to be waiting for me at my hotel, I can guarantee I wouldn't make it through this shindig tonight without disgracing myself. And I've got some early morning appointments tomorrow."

"I'll fly down if you want me," she offered softly.

"If I want you? Oh, God, babe . . . No, though I hate like hell to be away from you, you'd better stay put. Curl up with Nijinsky for tonight."

"And what will you curl up with?"

"X-rated fantasies about how we'll celebrate my homecoming. It'll be—damn! Look at the time! I've got to get a move on."

"I—I'm glad you called." She wanted to say so much more than that, but her feelings were too fragile, too tender to be fully articulated.

"Good night, Melissa. Sweet dreams, sweetheart."

The Thursday class with Yuri went better than Melissa had dared hope. The Russian dancer charmed her pupils with his droll, fractured English and unabashedly dazzled them with an elegant but athletic display of the flashiest leaps and jumps in his repertoire.

"Is most fun I am having in long time," Yuri announced afterward as they rode back to Lincoln Center in a taxi. Due to a late change in the MBT's schedule,

Yuri was performing that evening. "I am particularly liking that last thing. What did little girl call it? Buggy? *Nyet. Boogie*. That is very good to do."

Melissa smiled. As usual, she'd ended the class with a freestyle dancing spree. Normally the song selected for this part of the lesson was a matter of choice. For Yuri's appearance, however, she had conferred with Rita Perez about the best choice. Dismissing the possibility that they might be laying it on a bit too thick, they'd settled on something obvious but effective: the theme from *Rocky*. Melissa wondered fleetingly how Bruno Franchiese would react to the information that the MBT's premier danseur had spent the afternoon boogying to the title song from a movie about a boxer.

"You boogie better than anyone I know, Yuri," she chuckled. "I can't thank you enough for today."

He shrugged magnanimously. "Is no need to thank. Is very much pleasure to do this." He appeared to be mulling something over. "You should have more classes someday, Melissa," he declared suddenly. "You have the heart for teaching. Is rare gift."

"I—thank you, Yuri. What a lovely thing to say."

The cab racketed to a halt in front of the huge Lincoln Center plaza a few minutes later, pulling up behind a sleek black limousine. Melissa paid the driver. Yuri, with old-fashioned courtesy, assisted her out of the taxi, then slammed the door shut and waved the cabbie on his way.

There was an autumn chill in the late-afternoon air. Melissa thrust her hands into the pockets of the navy-blue pea jacket she had put on over her jeans, white cotton turtleneck, and cloud-gray angora sweater. The wind plucked at her dark hair.

"I really am grateful to you for coming to the class, Yuri," she said. "Especially since you've got to dance tonight."

"Yuri Alexandrovich does not disappoint." He grinned,

hefting his canvas dance tote. "Especially not beautiful ballerina. Besides, now you—what is saying? Ah! Now you owe me one. *Da?*"

"*Da.*" She kissed him on the cheek, laughing.

"You will come to performance tonight?"

"Well—" She hesitated, not realizing how her mouth suddenly softened and curved. "To tell the truth, I'm hoping I might have company tonight."

"I think that could be arranged, Melissa."

She whirled, startled, with the grace of a gazelle, flushing with both surprise and pleasure. "Sean!" she exclaimed. "I didn't expect you back so soon!"

"I hustled."

Rising up on tiptoe, her hands resting lightly on his broad chest, she kissed him on the mouth. His own hands closed around her waist as he returned the caress with devastating thoroughness. Her eyes were wide and shining when he released her.

"How—how did you know where to find me?" she asked breathlessly.

"I called Rita from the airport. She said you'd left the youth center in a cab and that she thought you and Mr. Volnoy were headed down to Lincoln Center. I took a chance and got lucky."

Melissa winced. She'd completely forgotten about Yuri in the excitement of seeing Sean. She turned back to the Russian dancer with a contrite expression. "Yuri, I'm sorry," she apologized. "This is my—my friend, Sean Culhane. Sean—Yuri Volnoy."

"Mr. Volnoy." The two men shook hands. "I'm an admirer of yours. I understand you made quite an impression with the uptown crowd today."

"Good impression, I am hoping. Please, as friend of Melissa's, you should be calling me Yuri."

"Thank you."

Yuri cocked his head quizzically. "Sean Culhane. I

think I have watched you on television program about American athletics. You are doing blow-by-blow descriptions of game of football."

Melissa managed to choke back a giggle. "That's play-by-play, Yuri," she corrected.

"Sorry." The Russian pulled a comic grimace. "Sometimes my English is not so good," he explained to Sean. "I am getting words confused. There was other day when I am talking to Melissa about coming off to her. Wrong, she says. What I should be saying is coming *on* to her."

"It sounds like a fascinating discussion."

"Yuri—"

"Was most fascinating," Yuri agreed. "You are knowing Melissa for many years?" he inquired.

"Yuri—" Melissa repeated. She was distinctly wary of the scampish look of speculation she saw dancing in Yuri's brown eyes. She had a rather good idea of what was going on inside his head, and she had no desire for it to come tumbling out of his mouth.

"Let's say Melissa and I recently decided to renew an old friendship," Sean returned coolly. "An...encore, if you will."

"Encore?" Yuri sampled the word, then nodded approvingly. "I am understanding. But now is time for me to go. Time to dance. Thankfully not with Emilie." He smiled at Melissa and winked. "Sadly, *dushka,* not with you. But soon, maybe, I hope. Sean Culhane, is honor to meet friend of Melissa and champion of throwing the pork skin." With a cheerful nod of farewell he turned and moved off, a jaunty bounce to his distinctive, turned-out-toe walk.

"Pork skin?" Sean repeated in a dubious undertone.

This time Melissa didn't even try to hold back the laughter. She leaned against Sean helplessly, relishing the strength of his lean body. "I th-think he meant p-pigskin," she sputtered. "As he said—"

"Sometimes his English is not so good. Yeah, I heard."

She looked up at him. "I'm very glad you hustled," she told him softly. "I missed you."

He traced the delicate fullness of her lips with one finger, his green-gold gaze darkening to jade. "I missed you, too," he assured her. "And if you don't stop looking at me with those silver-smoke eyes of yours, I may be tempted to demonstrate just how much right here, right now."

She smiled teasingly. "What's preventing you?"

His tawny brows rose. "For one thing, it would shock the hell out of the chauffeur."

"You have a chauffeur?"

"And something for him to drive." He indicated the glossy black limousine by the curb. "It's big enough for two. You want a ride?"

"I live only three blocks from here," she reminded him, allowing herself to be ushered over to the car. A polite-faced driver in an impeccably tailored uniform opened the door.

"We'll take the scenic route," Sean promised, handing her in to the luxurious wine and black interior. As she scooted across the expensive leather upholstery, her fingers drifting over its buttery-soft surface, he slid in after her. The door closed shut behind him.

"I have friends whose apartments are smaller than this," she said, glancing around. There was a compact, elegantly appointed bar, a multibuttoned executive phone, and even a small built-in television set. An opaque partition separated the driver from the passengers. The windows were tinted a smoky tone that shielded the car's occupants from prying eyes. The sense of privacy was complete . . . and provocative.

"I use it for business."

"Ummm." She shifted toward him. "Speaking of which, how was your trip?" She felt the smooth acceleration as the car pulled away from the curb and wondered briefly if Sean was really taking her back to her apartment. She decided she didn't care. "You look a little tired." There was an odd air of strain about him.

Sean unbuttoned his gray pinstripe jacket and loosened the knot of his tie with an impatient gesture. "I haven't been sleeping well. You, on the other hand, sweetheart, look as though you've been enjoying at least eight hours of innocent dreams a night."

Melissa flushed. She'd had plenty of dreams during Sean's absence, but none of them remotely qualified for the description "innocent." "Thank you. I think."

"It was a compliment. Volnoy was right."

"Yuri?"

"You said on the phone the other night he'd told you you had a glow." He didn't sound pleased.

Melissa swept her ebony fall of hair back over her shoulder. "Well, I don't suppose I can take all the credit for that," she said softly. Very delicately she began to walk her slender fingers up his arm. She wanted Sean to kiss her again . . . to touch her. The closed-in feeling of the car made her acutely aware of the utter maleness of him. He'd been much the man when she'd known him five years before, but there was a new maturity, a tempered potency, to him now that stirred her to her very core. "Do you suppose," she said with a husky catch in her voice, "that it would shock your chauffeur if I demonstrated how much I missed you?"

He trapped her wandering fingers with one hand and turned to face her directly. "What was that he called you back there?" he demanded abruptly.

Melissa blinked, recognizing the snap of leashed temper in his green-gold eyes. "I don't—what Yuri called me?"

He nodded. *"Dushka,* wasn't it? Is that a pet name?"

"Oh—" She relaxed. "It's Russian for darling."

Sean let go of her. "I see."

A fine line of puzzlement marred the ivory skin of

her smooth brow. "Sean, Yuri calls everyone *dushka,*" she explained reasonably.

"I'm thrilled to hear it." He leaned forward and opened the bar. "Do you want a drink?"

"No, I don't! I want to know why you're—" Her eyes widened in shocked disbelief. "Sean Culhane, are you *jealous?*"

He withdrew his fingers from the bottle he'd reached for and looked at her. "You don't have to sound so damned pleased about it."

"I'm not," she stated clearly. "I mean, I suppose I am in a way." She hesitated, honest enough to admit to herself that she was *very* pleased. "But there's no reason for you to be jealous of Yuri." She met his gaze briefly, then dropped her eyes.

He slipped his hand under her chin and tilted her face up. "That first day at lunch, after your appointment with Dave Goldberg, you told me Yuri Volnoy was special."

"You said the same thing about Rita Perez," she reminded him. "Look, Yuri sees me as a dancing partner. That's all. He's not interested in me that—other way."

His expression changed as his other hand came up to trace the beautiful curve of her cheek and jaw. "A man would have to be gay, blind, or dead not to be interested in you that 'other' way, Twinkletoes. And the last I heard, Leningrad's leotarded Lothario was straight, keen-eyed, and very much alive."

Melissa moistened her lips with the tip of her tongue, deliberately provoking the golden fire in his jungle-cat eyes. Slowly, with the boldness she had always reserved for her dancing roles, she slid her palms up the broad expanse of his chest. Deftly she finished undoing his tie. After a fractional hesitation she undid the top button of his crisp white shirt.

"Perhaps I should have said I'm not interested in *him* that other way," she murmured, opening a second button.

"Then what were you doing talking to him about his coming on to you?" Sean's voice was not quite steady. So far he'd made no move to stop her. At the same time, he wasn't being very encouraging, either.

Her fingers trembled slightly as she proceeded to the third button. "You mean the other day? Actually Yuri was explaining why he hadn't even . . . you know." Button number four gave way. She leaned forward to press her lips against the well-muscled hair-rough triangle she had revealed.

Now Sean's hands moved, closing over her slim shoulders, holding her at arm's length. Her gray eyes clouded with anxious frustration. "Just what was his explanation?" he asked, the dimple at the corner of his mouth very much in evidence.

"Well—" She flushed. "What it boils down to is that Yuri thinks it's sexier to be with me onstage than off."

Sean stared at her for a few seconds, then started to chuckle. "If he truly believes that, he's got a problem that goes way beyond being weak in English."

"Oh, really?" she challenged. "Whatever do you— mmmm, Sean—"

The hands that had been holding her at a distance now gathered her close. Closing her eyes, Melissa blissfully gave herself up to a slow, hungry kiss. Their lips met, moved, fused, then moved again. She flicked her tongue teasingly against his as it delved with searching skill into the sweetness of her mouth. Possessively her hands roved up his bare chest. She could feel the change in his breathing as he responded to her touch.

"God, I've wanted you so badly these last few days, I've hurt with it," he muttered, nuzzling the side of her neck. "I kept thinking about you and me together Sunday night after the game."

"And Monday morning . . . after Sunday night—" she breathed, nipping softly at his earlobe. "When you taught me the new position—"

"There are plenty more where that came from." He'd opened up the front of her pea jacket and slipped his hands up under the angora sweater. He fondled her breasts with erotic expertise through the thin fabric of her cotton pullover, playing with the stiffening peaks with blood-heating results. Melissa felt as though her very essence were melting into liquid flame. "I sure as hell hope you're not wearing a leotard, Melissa," he said thickly.

"I'm not," she replied unnecessarily. Even as she spoke, he was tugging the turtleneck free from the waistband of her snug-fitting jeans. She arched up instinctively to make his task easier, trembling as his fingers stroked over the satiny skin of her torso. She reciprocated by opening the final buttons of her shirt, then pulling it loose.

Somehow in the next few moments he managed to shed his jacket and tie and she found herself eased deftly out of her pea coat and sweater. Sean pressed her down against the seat, his mouth covering hers, exploring and cherishing with increasing demand.

"Volnoy can have you onstage," he declared hoarsely. "But I want you once the curtain goes down."

"A command performance?" She looked up at him with passion-clouded eyes, the pale oval of her face framed in a raven-dark tumble of glossy hair.

He kissed the throbbing pulse at the base of her throat. A fever had taken possession of both of them. "Have you ever made love in a limousine?" he whispered into her ear.

Melissa shook her head. "I've never even ridden in a limousine before. But wh-what about the d-driver?"

Sean shifted and reached for the phone she had noticed earlier. His free hand moved to the snap at the top of her jeans as he put the receiver to his ear.

"Emory," he said with admirable control. "We'd like to take a run out to the airport and back. What? No. Kennedy, it's farther out. That's right. No, no problem.

This just happens to be Miss Stewart's first time in a limo, and I'd like her to have enough time to enjoy the experience. I'll leave the route to you. Thank you."

CHAPTER SEVEN

"LAURETTE, WHAT AM I going to do?" Melissa asked, her delicately featured face growing serious. She set down her fork and pushed away the remainder of her avocado vinaigrette.

They were having a late lunch at O'Neal's Baloon, a popular restaurant located across the street from Lincoln Center. The place was active and noisy, and a jumble of wooden tables, red chairs, Tiffany lamps, posters, and vaguely artsy patrons. It was a place to gossip, flirt, commiserate, and indulge in anything from a predate drink to a posttheater snack to a solid three-course dinner.

Laurette surveyed her friend thoughtfully. "Why do you have to 'do' anything?" she inquired. "Judging by the way you look, everything's terrific."

Melissa sighed. Her hair was styled in a glossy coronet of braids and she was wearing a demurely old-fashioned moss green wool dress she'd found on sale at Laura

113

Ashley. But there was a very modern sensuality about her. It wasn't anything blatant, yet it surrounded her with a subtle aura, like a hauntingly rare perfume.

"Everything *is* terrific," she conceded. "To a point. Dr. Goldberg says my knee is going to be fine. I've been taking a daily class for more than a week now with no problems. Of course it's going to be some time before I'm back to performing."

"You'll be back soon and you'll be great."

"Thanks. The coaching is turning out better than I expected, too. And the teaching at the youth center—" Melissa's gray eyes sparkled like silvery gems. "Did I tell you about the audition I arranged for Tonio Martinez?"

"Several times."

"Oh." Melissa gave a fleetingly apologetic smile. "It's just that I'm so proud of him. I'm sure he'll be accepted by the school. The only problem is money. He's got to get that scholarship!"

"Melissa." Laurette's hazel eyes were knowing.

"I'm babbling."

"No, you're avoiding the issue."

"It's just—oh, God, Laurette, I'm in love with him."

"'Him' being Sean Culhane, I take it."

"Of course!" She'd known for weeks and the knowledge both thrilled and terrified her. She'd loved him five years ago, and what had it gotten her?

"Just checking, sweetie. In love, hmmm? Well, I had a feeling it wasn't just unbridled animal passion. Although I'm willing to bet that if there were a Super Bowl of sex, Sean Culhane would be on the first string."

"Laurette!"

Heaven knew, it would be easier if it *were* just unbridled animal passion. She'd tried to convince herself that all she felt for Sean was physical attraction, but it had been a losing battle. Yuri Volnoy had hit the nail perceptively on the head when he'd contrasted his light-

hearted attitude toward lovemaking with her own. And
her mother had known, too.

"You're making the same mistake I did!" Verna Stewart had warned, her face tight. "You can't separate sex
from love. Men can. I was in love once, and look at me
now! I'm old and alone. Please, darling, listen to your
mother. You have a chance to do all the things I wasn't
able to. . . ."

A pained look flickered across Melissa's face, rippling
the dove gray of her eyes as an errant breeze might disturb
the serene surface of a lake.

"Forgive the prurient speculation," the redhead apologized. "Actually it's envy, pure and simple. Well, maybe
not so pure . . ." Her voice trailed off and she frowned.
"You've really got it bad, haven't you?"

"Yes," Melissa admitted flatly. She toyed with a packet
of crackers from the breadbasket on the table. "I wish I
could just . . . just . . ."

"Lie back and enjoy it?"

Melissa gave a small mirthless laugh. "Something like
that." She worried her lower lip with her teeth. "I don't
know what to do."

"So you said. At the risk of repeating myself, why
do you have to do *anything?* If you were in the throes
of an unrequited love affair, that would be one thing.
But your gorgeous hunk of an ex-jock is obviously nuts
about you. Lord, honey, that day at the fountain, his
eyes were all over you! And my well-honed instincts tell
me he's the type who likes to touch as well as look. So
what's the problem?"

"My dancing." Melissa reduced a cracker to crumbs.

"Huh?"

"I'm scared about what's going to happen when I go
back to work."

"Whoa. I think I missed something. You think you're
going to put on your pointe shoes and he's going to take
a powder?"

"I don't know what I think! But, Laurette, I'm so afraid it's going to be five years ago all over again. I'm going to start dancing and I'm going to lose him."

"And you don't want to do that. Lose him, I mean."

"No, I don't." Melissa's voice was stark.

Laurette fiddled restlessly with a napkin. "You mentioned five years ago. That's when you and he—"

"Don't tell me you haven't gotten all the details from the company grapevine."

"We-e-e-ll . . ."

"We had an affair," Melissa said. "We were going to get married."

"Married?" Laurette leaned forward with more eagerness than grace. She almost knocked over a water glass. "My God, *that* I hadn't heard."

"The engagement was very . . . informal. It lasted only a few days. We didn't have time to announce it." They hadn't even had time to pick out a ring. Sean had given her his Super Bowl ring. She'd flung it—and a torrent of angry, agonized words—in his face the night of their final quarrel.

"What happened?"

"AfterImages."

Laurette blinked. "The ballet Franchiese made you famous with? The role he created just for you? I don't get it."

Melissa swallowed. "Sean asked me to marry him just a few days after I was cast in *AfterImages*. He didn't want to wait. Neither did I. Not at first. Then I realized there was going to be so much—rehearsals, preparations, all the extra work with Mr. Franchiese. I—I asked Sean if we could wait and get married after the debut of the ballet."

"And he said no?"

He'd said no . . . and a great many other things.

"What do you want of me?" she cried, astonished by the sudden savagery of his temper.

"I want to marry you!" he'd snapped furiously.

"And I want to marry you. But this ballet—"

"This ballet! This ballet is just an excuse, Melissa. Why don't you admit it? After the gala debut of *AfterImages* I'm sure you'll come up with some other reason to delay the wedding. The MBT tour. Or maybe a guest appearance with some visiting company. You're going to be Franchiese's new star. The priestess on pointe, wedded to her art! I suppose the prospects of becoming Mrs. Sean Culhane seem pretty earthbound compared to that."

"I'm a dancer!"

"*I am a dancer!* That's the bottom line, isn't it, sweetheart. My biggest mistake was thinking you were a woman, too."

She wanted desperately to be both—for herself as well as for him. The problem was that while she knew and understood Melissa Stewart the dancer, Melissa Stewart the woman was still an often elusive stranger. The only times she was absolutely certain of her existence were when she was in Sean's arms.

"Melissa?" Laurette asked, concerned.

Melissa shook her head quickly. The memory still ripped into her like a knife. "I—yes . . . yes. Sean said no to the idea of waiting to get married."

The redhead made a face, clearly debating something with herself. "Look, sugarplum, I can see you're hurting over this, but let me ask you something. Was it your idea to ask Sean to postpone the wedding?"

"Of cour—" The automatic affirmation died in her throat. "My—my mother was against our getting married so quickly," she conceded quietly.

"I see." Laurette's brows rose pointedly.

"Not you, too!"

"What?"

"Sean's always tried to cast my mother as some kind of—oh—wicked witch or something. Yes, she pushed

me into dancing. And yes, she was ambitious for me.
But a lot of parents are like that. She wanted what was
best for me.''

"She wanted what *she* thought was best for you,''
Laurette corrected bluntly. "Okay, Melissa, I hate to
speak ill of the dead and all that, but there are ballet
mothers and there are ballet mothers. Yours was really
obsessed by your career.''

"But—" Melissa instinctively began to protest.

"It's the truth, hon. You know, I sometimes had the
feeling the only reason she didn't mind you and me being
friends was because she knew I was never going to be
any competition for you.''

"But you're very good!''

Laurette shrugged. "Sure I am. But I'm not as good
as you are.'' She paused. "Look, when I first met you I
thought you had to be the biggest phony in the world. I
mean, I couldn't believe anybody with your talent could
be anything but a bitch. But no, instead of coming on
like a prima donna, you were little Miss Sweetness and
Light. I figured it had to be an act until the kids in the
corps set me straight. Even the ones who were eaten up
with envy said you were a genuinely nice person. They
also said you didn't need to stab anyone in the back
because your mother would do it for you.''

The color drained out of Melissa's face. "My mother
never did anything like that,'' she exclaimed, appalled.

"Maybe not literally, but from where I stood it always
seemed very clear she wasn't going to let anything or
anybody get in the way of your making it to the top.''

Oh, Mama, Melissa thought. What did I let you do
to me? What did I let you do to yourself? She drew a
shaky breath before she spoke.

"Maybe . . . maybe what you say is true. But my mother's gone now. And what she did or didn't do is in the
past. It doesn't matter. What does matter is my dancing
and the fact that I don't think Sean can accept it.''

Laurette reached daintily for one of the slices of rich green avocado left on Melissa's plate. She munched it down, licking the thick mustardy vinaigrette sauce from her fingers. "He could be jealous," she suggested.

"Jealous?"

"Sure," Laurette nodded. "You're a star, right? You've got fame, fortune—"

"Laurette, Laurette. Sean Culhane has more fame and fortune than I'll ever have. Stop a hundred people on the street and mention my name and all you'll get are blank looks. Mention Lion Culhane and I promise you'll get swoons from the women and sports stories from the men."

"But he's retired."

"Right. He's retired to the cover of *Fortune* magazine because of the family fitness center concept he's financed and to a lead article in *TV Guide* because of his sports-casting."

"I get your point. Okay. So he's not jealous. Is he pushing you for a commitment? You said he wanted to marry you before. Has he brought that up again?"

Melissa lowered her eyes. Except for the biting references to his proposal that first day after he'd taken her to lunch, there'd been no talk of marriage.

He wanted her. He'd made that plainly, pleasurably, clear. Sexually Sean had placed his brand on her, and she sensed the ecstasy of their physical merging was as irresistible to him as it was to her. Beyond that . . .

What was it he'd said that day? That he was willing to "settle" for what he could get. Was that what he was doing? Or, after five years, was an affair all he wanted?

Perhaps *she* was the one who was going to have to settle for what *she* could get.

"Melissa?" Laurette snapped her fingers. "Yoo-hoo, Sleeping Beauty."

Melissa blinked. "No," she said. "He hasn't—he isn't pushing for anything." Why should he?

"Then, for Pete's sake, don't worry about it!" the

redhead urged. "At least don't worry about it now. If you and Sean wind up breaking up again, well, damn few things last forever. And just remember, whatever went wrong between you two five years ago, you've still managed to get back together for a return engage—ah—for an encore."

Melissa made a wry face. "When Mr. Franchiese told me to have an affair, I don't think this is what he had in mind."

"Definitely not," Laurette agreed.

It was not in Melissa Stewart's nature to deliberately provoke a confrontation. She wasn't an emotional coward; indeed, she had a serene strength of character that surprised those who assumed she was as fragile as her ethereal appearance suggested. But while she'd learned to stand her ground, her inclination was to hold back rather than to reach out when she was uncertain.

And she was uncertain about Sean. Very uncertain.

So, with a half-eager, half-anxious awareness of the rapidly passing days of her exile from dancing, she kept her deepest fears and feelings to herself and decided to follow Laurette's cynically sensible counsel. She'd enjoy what she had with Sean for as long as she had it.

"Look, Twinkletoes," Sean teased her several days later over dinner. "When I asked you to pick the restaurant, I thought you'd at least come up with a place where they cook the food."

Melissa paused in the act of transferring a morsel of seaweed-wrapped zucchini and rice from an antique lacquered tray to her mouth. "Don't you like raw squid?"

"Is that what this is?" he countered with a boyish grin as he poked a silky white tidbit of something with a pair of deftly wielded chopsticks.

"Actually, that's eel." She smiled her thanks to the prettily kimonoed waitress who glided to their table and gracefully refreshed their bowls of tea. The young woman gave a cheerful little nod, then moved away, her manner as soothingly calm as the elegant Oriental simplicity of the restaurant's decor.

"Eel, hmmm?" Sean echoed. Dressed in a three-piece tailored suit of tobacco brown, he radiated sophisticated authority. Despite his banter about the food, his dexterous handling of the Oriental eating utensils indicated his familiarity with exotic cuisine. Melissa found herself momentarily fascinated by his hands; the long lean fingers and the powerful palms evoked a secret thrill in her. They were slightly callused from the tennis and handball he played regularly. The hint of roughness always felt erotic against her sensitive skin.

The discreet glint of his Super Bowl ring snapped her out of her reverie.

"If you don't want the eel, try some shrimp," she suggested with an innocent smile.

One tawny brow quirked upward and a knowing gleam flashed in the changeable green-gold eyes. "Ah, yes...shrimp. With the heads still on, I see. A nice touch, sweetheart. I've always had a perverse fondness for having my food look back at me."

Melissa busied herself selecting and then savoring a portion of ruby-red tuna and vinegared rice. The subtle contrast of taste and texture lingered pleasantly on her tongue. She took a sip of green tea and then looked across at Sean.

"I think the heads are supposed to have some sort of aphrodisiac powers," she told him demurely.

"Indeed?" he drawled. "To tell the truth, sweetheart, I don't need shrimp heads. Now, if you can come up with something for acute exhaustion—"

"Perhaps you should try getting to bed earlier?" She tossed her hair back with a graceful movement. Silver and crystal earrings sparkled on the lobes of her ears.

She was wearing a chemise dress of smoke-gray chiffon. It gave the provocative impression that it might vanish in a strong breeze, leaving her naked.

"Going to bed isn't the problem," Sean retorted. "It's getting to sleep, my insatiable little darling. It beats me how you can sit there looking so dewy-eyed and fresh after you had me up till all hours last night. To say nothing of what went on early this morning."

"I could say a lot about that."

"I'll just bet you could. For the record, though, we're going to have to have a serious discussion with your cat about who's in charge around your apartment."

"Poor Nijinsky. It really wasn't his fault. You were sleeping on his side of the bed, after all."

"*My* side now, babe. Haven't you heard that the lion has a very strong territorial instinct?"

"Now that you mention it—" Her gray eyes danced with quicksilver amusement and she felt a quiver of pleasure at the possessiveness in his tone. "Still, it was pretty funny."

"Oh, hilarious. One minute I'm making love with you and the next I'm contending with a cat who's doing a damn good imitation of an all-pro tackle I once tangled with. I don't mind the occasional fingernail scratch on my shoulders, Melissa, but I draw the line at genuine claw marks down my back. It's hard to explain at the health club."

She flushed delicately. "I told you Nijinsky was attack-trained."

"Hmmm." Sean picked up a shrimp and popped it into his mouth. "Look, while we're on the subject of your faithful feline, how do you suppose he'd react if you went away with me for a weekend?"

Melissa set her chopsticks down. "What?"

"I've got to go out to L.A. next weekend for the network. It's not going to be much of a game. The way the other team's been playing, they'll probably give up eight or nine touchdowns before the end of the first quarter. L.A. could send in their cheerleaders and win."

"You're going to be doing blow-by-blow commentary?" she asked, recalling Yuri's fractured phraseology.

"That's right. Instead of throwing the old pork skin, I'll be tossing around statistics about pass completions and yardage gained."

"But if you're going to be working—"

"There'll be plenty of time for us," he promised, the caressingly sensual note in his voice telling her exactly how some of that time would be spent.

"Well—" she began hesitatingly.

"Please. It's not as though I'm asking you to miss a performance, Melissa. Besides, I'd like you to see what I do."

Was there an edge of reproach in his voice? Several times during their previous relationship he'd asked her to be his guest at an out-of-town game, but she'd always refused. There had been too many scheduling conflicts. They'd quarreled over the situation more than once. As a result, she'd seen him play football only in a handful of home games.

"I'd like to go with you," she said with quiet sincerity. "And I think Nijinsky will survive the separation without trauma. I'll ask Laurette to take care of him. She's got a cat, too. A Siamese named Bruce Lee."

"Wonderful. Nijinsky can pick up some martial arts pointers." He took a swallow of his tea, an odd look passing over his face. His brows came together. "You didn't have any plans for next weekend, did you?" he asked suddenly. "I didn't really think—that is, I know you've been busy these last few weeks..." He let the sentence dangle, unfinished and ambiguous.

Melissa experienced a peculiar flutter of anxiety. She had been keeping busy. Beyond the lessons at the youth center, she was assisting at the MBT school and coaching two soloists besides Dianne Kelso. She'd also been roped into helping the company's fund-raisers in their never-ending search for money.

She still missed the act of dancing desperately, of course, although not as desperately as she'd feared. Her return to daily classes—carefully limited by Dr. Goldberg's repeated warnings about her knee—had helped satisfy her ingrained hunger for music and movement.

She sighed suddenly. Three weeks until she could go back fully to "her" world. And then what?

"Melissa?" Sean's voice was sharp, almost challenging.

"No, I didn't have any plans."

Their waitress reappeared at that moment and quickly cleared the table. Once their entree plates were removed she graciously set out a platter of fresh fruits, sliced with lapidary precision and artfully arranged on crushed ice. That done, she glided off once more.

"The MBT's going to be doing *AfterImages* next Saturday, aren't they?"

"That's right. Dianne Kelso and Rex Castleberry are dancing." God, what was he trying to do?

"How do you feel, having her do that role?"

Her eyes widened in surprise at the apparent insensitivity of the question. "How do you think I feel?"

"That's what I want to know," he returned evenly. "Look, I know what I went through that season I sat out because of my shoulder and had to watch Brewer playing instead of me. I yelled myself hoarse, since we were teammates. I also envied him so much I could taste it."

"So?"

"So maybe I have some idea of what you're feeling. But that ballet . . . hell, it was bad enough seeing Brewer throw the passes that should have been mine. Still, it wasn't like he was running plays that had been created especially for me."

Melissa searched his face for several seconds, trying to find some clue to the motive for this line of questioning. Was he trying to goad her into an admission of how much ballet meant to her? Was he looking for a hint that after five years she regretted the decision she'd made? Or was he just possibly making an effort to understand her world and its demands?

"I guess it makes a difference when you have a choreographer, not a coach, behind you," she said with tentative humor, then grew thoughtful. "It is hard having someone else dance the role Mr. Franchiese made for me. The first time it happened I was so jealous I couldn't see straight. And I know it was bitchy, but I was glad the dancer taking the part—Stephanie Chaplin—didn't get as good reviews as I did in the role."

"Do you read your reviews?"

"Sometimes. But I don't need a critic to tell me whether my dancing is right or wrong. My—my mother always read them. She used to keep a scrapbook of them." In her mind's eye Melissa could see Verna Stewart slowly leafing through the leather-covered binders she'd so painstakingly prepared, lingering hungrily over the pictures, the programs, and the newspaper articles. Melissa had looked through the scrapbooks once after her mother's death, then stored them away.

Sean nodded. "About next weekend. If you hadn't hurt your knee, would you—"

She regarded him with a flash of defiance. "If I hadn't hurt my knee, I'd be dancing *AfterImages,* yes. And I wouldn't be going to Los Angeles with you."

But you'd wish you were, a small voice inside her whispered with the simplicity of utter certainty.

There was a long silence. Five years ago, Melissa thought with an ache, there would have been an explosion. But now . . . now, perhaps, Sean didn't care enough to explode.

His next words, quietly spoken, made her tremble. "If you were dancing, I wouldn't have asked you to come."

CHAPTER EIGHT

BEING KISSED AWAKE, Melissa thought with a delicious sense of drowsiness, was infinitely preferable to being shocked into a state of awareness by the shrilling of an alarm clock. With languidly sensual responsiveness she shifted her warmly pliant body, offering herself willingly to the teasingly skillful caresses that were beginning to rouse her even in her slumberous condition.

A puff of warm breath fanned her sleep-flushed cheek. Strong but gentle fingers stroked aside the dark tumble of hair that veiled part of her face. She gave a shivery sigh, the muscles of her stomach tightening in pleasurable anticipation as teeth nipped carefully at the lobe of one of her ears.

"This is your wake-up call, Miss Stewart," Sean murmured, low and husky. "It's now 8:03."

"Mmm," she breathed. *If I don't open my eyes,* she

thought with childish superstition, *I can make this moment last forever*.

"Rise and shine, Twinkletoes." He sounded amused. She felt the faint rasp of his overnight growth of beard as he began to nibble his way along the sensitive cord of her throat.

"I'm having the most wonderful ... dream. . . ."

"Dream, hmmm? Let's see what we can do to make it a little sweeter."

Melissa arched in shocked pleasure, her eyes flying open as his fingers found her with unerringly intimate expertise. "Se-Sean!" she gasped, staring up at him.

"I always suspected it would take more than a kiss to get Sleeping Beauty to wake up," he commented provocatively, the dimple at the corner of his mobile mouth very much in evidence as he surveyed her.

She took a shuddery breath, allowing the exquisite explosion of sensation he had triggered within her with that one sure touch to dissipate. The drowsy softness of her dove-colored eyes took on a quicksilver sparkle, and her lips curved into an enchanting, daring smile.

"And now that Sleeping Beauty's awake?" she prompted. Reaching up, she traced the strong, slightly stubborn line of his jaw with a slow, lazy finger, relishing the prickly bristle she discovered there. When she reached his chin she began to mark an equally deliberate path down his throat, through the crisp mat of tawny chest hair to the tautly muscled plain of his . . .

He stayed her hand. "That depends on whether Her Highness has a desire to be caught *flagrante delicto* when room service delivers breakfast."

"*Flagrante delicto*. Is that another one of those positions I never learned in ballet class?"

"Something like that." His eyes darkened to a glinting jade. Her soft lips parted eagerly on a blissful sigh as, releasing her hand, he bent his head and brought his mouth down on hers.

Tenderly, without urgency, they sought and savored each other. She teased and tempted his tongue with her own, yielding willingly when he responded with a leisurely exploration of her mouth. Beneath the sheets his hands fondled and stroked, drawing a swift response in the peaking of her rosy nipples, kindling a sweet, glowing warmth.

The fingers of one of her hands tangled in the thickness of his hair, softer, much softer than a lion's mane, for all its tawny color. Her other hand drifted over the sleek power of his broad shoulders to his back, feeling the smooth play of his muscles beneath the tanned sheath of skin.

"Melissa—" he said hoarsely, breaking the kiss with visible reluctance.

"Yes?"

"I meant what I said about room service. I ordered breakfast for a quarter to nine."

"You can think of food at a time like this?"

"What can I say, sweetheart? I'm a victim of my appetites—all of them." He grinned and dropped a light kiss on her nose. "Besides, I work better on a full stomach."

"You also weigh more," she pointed out, wriggling away from him and sitting up. She flicked her ebony fall of hair back over her shoulders.

"You weren't complaining about my weight last night," he drawled softly, running a casual finger down the ivory smoothness of her spine.

Shifting away, she draped the sheet around her and favored him with a haughty glance. Neither of them had complained about anything the night before.

They'd arrived in Los Angeles after a first-class transcontinental flight. A cheerful gofer from the network had greeted them at the airport and driven them to the stunningly futuristic Bonaventure Hotel, where they were staying. Naturally sensitive to visual beauty, Melissa had been amazed by the spectacular creation of architect John Portman. The five golden towers of the hotel glistened in the Los Angeles skyline like some extraordinary gilded fantasy.

The simple act of checking into the hotel together— it was the first time they had ever done such a thing— had set off an electric reaction between them. Melissa felt her bones turn to liquid when Sean casually slipped his arm about her waist as they entered the glass-walled elevator that would take them to their room. She hadn't dared look at him, but she'd known from the tension in his body that he shared her excitement.

The demands of Sean's network duties caused a delay of many agonizing hours between the time they checked in and the time they finally acted on the desire that was firing both of them. Finally alone, they'd made love with a driving, sexual hunger, the rhythm of their passion quickening with each heartbeat, each gasping breath. Later they had come together again, this time with slow, lingering movements, subtly rousing caresses, and softly murmured endearments.

"I wasn't complaining, Sean, because I couldn't," Melissa said with an assumed air of dignity. The skin of her back was tingling from the abstract designs he was sketching lazily on it with his finger.

"Is that so?"

"Yes, that's so. You were practically squashing me." She tried unsuccessfully to control the delicious tremor of pleasure that ran through her slim body. "I've always wondered what it felt like to be the player on the bottom of one of those big pile-ups of bodies on a football field. Now I know."

Chuckling, Sean sat up and ran a hand through his thick golden-brown hair. He pressed his mouth briefly to the silken curve of her naked shoulder. "I'll tell you what, dearest," he said huskily. "Next time you get to tackle me. Okay?"

"Well—"

"And since I'm such a good sport, I won't remind you about all those illegal holds you were using last night."

"Sean!"

"But I will tell you you have the best backfield motion it's ever been my pleasure to—hey!"

Melissa had hit him in the face with a pillow. A split-second later he tumbled her back against the mattress.

My God, she thought with dizzy exhilaration, talk about quick hands—

"Time out!" she squealed.

"No."

"Off-sides?" she offered, her voice going up.

"Sorry. This is one quarterback sack that's not—"

The knock that interrupted them was brief and discreet, but they both froze with almost comic suddenness. Sean groaned with a mixture of frustration and resigned comprehension.

"Damn!" he swore under his breath, releasing her.

"Don't glare at me," she threw at him, her eyes dancing impudently and her dark brows rising. "You're the one who ordered food."

"I've got to keep up my energy somehow, you little witch," he countered.

There was another knock at the door. It was a bit firmer this time.

"Room service, sir," a pleasant male voice announced.

Smiling in demure triumph, Melissa slipped off the bed and walked nonchalantly into the bathroom. "Be nice to the waiter," she tossed over her shoulder as she made her graceful exit. "It's not his fault you can't control your appetites!"

She waited five minutes before returning. In that time she vigorously brushed her hair, splashed some cool water on her face, and, for want of her own dressing gown, donned the dark-blue bathrobe Sean had left on the hook on the back of the door. It was the same robe he had given her to wear that first night at his apartment. She cuddled the oversized garment around her.

Yuri was right, she thought, staring at herself in the mirror. *I do have a glow. I look like . . . a woman in love.*

Did Sean know how she felt about him? Did it matter to him? Would he accept her love as something to be cherished and nurtured? Or would he use it as a tool with which to pry her away from her other love, the ballet?

Did he love her?

Giving her hair a final pat, Melissa drew herself erect in a supple movement and opened the bathroom door. Taking a deep breath, she walked back into the earth-toned bedroom.

"Did you order anything for me?" she inquired lightly.

Clad only in a pair of tan cord jeans, Sean was sitting at a well-laden table evidently set up by the room service waiter. He forked up a mouthful of scrambled eggs with relish. "I may be able to spare you a few crumbs," he grinned. "Provided you apologize for that sneak attack with the pillow."

"I was provoked!" she protested, taking the rattan seat opposite him at the table.

"Provoked?" He handed her a coffee cup.

"That remark about my backfield motion." Picking up the coffeepot, she served herself a portion of the fragrant steaming brew.

"That was supposed to be a compliment."

"Oh, really?"

"Um-hm. And that strategic streak you made to the bathroom a few minutes ago only reinforces my opinion about—"

"Never mind!"

"Anything you say," he said mildly, his green-gold eyes clearly signaling his amusement.

They breakfasted companionably, with Melissa con-

fining herself to coffee, a large glass of iced, freshly
squeezed orange juice, and an oven-warm croissant. She
licked the crumbs of the flaky buttery-rich roll from her
fingers with undisguised enjoyment.

"So . . ." she said, smiling with satisfaction. "You have
to go out to the stadium this morning?"

"That's right." Sean finished his coffee. Dropping his
linen napkin on the table, he rose and stretched with
controlled catlike grace. "The network's still trying to
straighten out some bugs in the new computer statistics
and graphics system, so they want to do another dry run.
I also want to do some scouting around about this new
offensive strategy L.A.'s been running." He crossed to
the luggage stand, where the bell captain had placed his
canvas and leather suitcase. Opening it, he pulled out an
eggshell-colored turtleneck and tugged it on. "Do you
have any plans?" he asked when his head emerged. The
top fit snugly, emphasizing the taut muscling of his torso
and the classic power of his shoulders.

"I thought—I thought I might do some window-
shopping," Melissa answered. She refolded her napkin
with painstaking care. "I've heard so much about the
fabulous Rodeo Drive, I'd like to see it."

Sean had turned his back to her and was pulling a
dark-chocolate suede jacket from the closet. "Do you
want any money?" he inquired casually.

For a moment Melissa didn't believe she'd heard him
correctly. The question was like an unexpected slap in
the face.

"No," she said tightly. "I don't want any money. I
don't need any either."

"Melissa—"

"I realize that when you first knew me five years ago
my salary barely put me above poverty level," she went
on. "I mean, it's no secret that the average MBT dancer
makes about half what the average stagehand does. But
I'm earning a comfortable living now that I'm a principal

with the company. Of course it's a pittance compared with what you—"

"Melissa!" he repeated sharply, cutting her off. He was facing her again, his expression rueful. She regarded him silently, her chin tilted with a hint of challenge. "It was a stupid, thoughtless thing to ask," he said quietly. "I apologize. But, believe me, I wasn't trying to be insulting. I just thought—" He shook his head. "Never mind. I *am* sorry."

There was a pause. Gray eyes searching green ones for a few long moments.

"Apology accepted," Melissa said eventually, getting up from the table. "I shouldn't have snapped at you. It's just that money has been such a touchy issue lately around the MBT, especially since there's talk that at least one of the other big dance companies is going to go out on strike over salaries."

He nodded his understanding, watching her intently for several seconds. "Five years ago you didn't care very much about that sort of thing," he commented neutrally.

"Five years ago I didn't know very much," she replied, aware that the conversation had taken on a double-edged quality. "Mama . . . my mother took care of the practical side of things. I was basically . . . oblivious." She gave a little laugh, combing her slender fingers slowly through her dusky tumble of hair. "You know, when I was first promoted to soloist it never even occurred to me that I'd be getting a raise. I was so overwhelmed by the honor . . . to have Mr. Franchiese pick me over so many other talented dancers—" She shook her head wonderingly, as though she couldn't quite believe how unaware of life's realities she had once been. "When I got my first paycheck after the promotion I thought they'd made a mistake and given me too much money," she confessed.

He walked over to her. There was a curious look flickering deep in his eyes—unexpected tenderness and something else she couldn't quite interpret. He cupped her chin gently in one strong hand, his thumb stroking slowly down the alabaster purity of her cheek.

"I'm sorry," he apologized again, his voice very intent. "I know you're very proud of what you've done these last five years. You should be, Melissa. You have a tremendous talent."

The sincerity with which he spoke moved her deeply. Yet she thought she detected a reluctant sadness lurking in his words. Would he have preferred it, she wondered, if she had not had such a success since they parted?

"Thank you," she said quietly, her eyes cloud-soft. "It—it means a lot to me to hear you say that."

The touch of his lips when he claimed her mouth was feather-light, almost hesitant. It had none of the playful sensuality of their earlier encounter, none of the drugging desire of the night before. This kiss was very sweet and curiously solemn, as though it were a seal to some unspoken pledge. It reminded her, almost painfully, of the first time he had kissed her five years before.

"A man could become addicted to the taste of your mouth," Sean said huskily when he finally lifted his head. "To the scent of you . . . the feel of your skin. God, Melissa—"

"I know." She placed two fingers briefly against his lips. "I feel the same way about you, Sean."

They stood gazing at each other in aching silence for an unknowable amount of time. It could have been a few fractions of a second or several minutes. Melissa felt herself drowning . . . melting . . . in the searching turbulence of his eyes. She was bound to him by a gossamer-fine but unbreakable web of awareness.

I love you, I love you, she said deep in her heart.

Enough to give up your dancing? a tiny voice asked.

She stiffened. The sudden tension in her slender body would have gone unnoticed by almost anyone else, but she could tell by the sudden change in his expression that Sean saw it. The moment . . . the spell . . . was broken.

"I've got to go to work," he said, his hand dropping away from her face.

Melissa nodded. Rising up on tiptoe, she brushed a butterfly kiss on the corner of his mouth near the crease of his dimple. "I'll see you later."

His lips quirked. "You'll do more than see me, sweetheart."

Before going out to do some shopping, Melissa did a slow stretching workout. The exercise left her ivory-fair face flushed and her eyes sparkling with exertion. She could sense the beginning of a protest from some of her muscles, but overall she felt marvelous. Grasping the back of a chair, she dropped gracefully into one last plié, her spine straight, her head held proudly, and her high-arched feet perfectly turned out in second position. Her slender arm swept down and out in response to the music she carried inside her head.

She'd been to see Dave Goldberg Friday morning before she and Sean had flown out to Los Angeles. Although he'd gruffly advised that she remain off her knee for a full two months as he'd initially ordered, he'd reluctantly conceded under her questioning that she'd made a complete recovery and could begin dancing again anytime she wanted.

Melissa had said nothing about this to Sean; she'd been afraid of his reaction. Her own response to the news was troubling enough. She was bitterly torn by the knowledge that her return to the art she adored would probably mean the loss of the man she deeply loved.

Damn few things last forever, Laurette had said.

A dancer's life is very short, her mother had told her. It wasn't fair!

She spent a pleasant day by herself, treating herself to lunch at a small restaurant in the Rodeo Collection, an elegant retail complex in the heart of Bevery Hills's chic shopping district. The dining room and bar were done up in a soothing combination of rose and aqua. The clientele was female and fashionable. Most of the customers were obviously taking a respite from a day of shopping: glossy packages from Gucci, Hermès, Ted Lapidus, Saks Fifth Avenue, Tiffany's, and many other pricey establishments were tucked under a number of Lucite-topped tables.

There was a bag tucked under Melissa's table, too. It contained a negligee set she'd purchased at Bonwit's. She'd tried it on impulsively. The stocky saleswoman waiting on her had been openly and flatteringly envious of how she looked in it.

"You don't think it's a little..." Melissa had asked, staring in wonder at her reflection.

"Of course it is!" the woman declared forthrightly but with a hint of feminine conspiracy lurking in her eyes. "But it's subtle, too. Subtle and sexy. It was made for you."

"Well..." Melissa colored slightly.

"Believe me, any woman would kill to look like you do. Besides, pink is definitely your color."

When Melissa eventually returned to the hotel room she found Sean lounging comfortably on the bed. He was surrounded by file folders and a scattering of computer printouts. His tawny hair was damp, as though he had recently showered, and he was wearing his navy robe. The belt was only loosely tied, so the top gaped, revealing a large triangle of his chest. His long powerful legs, with the well-muscled calves and rock-hard thighs, were stretched out in front of him as he leaned back against the stack of pillows he had propped against the headboard. Melissa recalled the feel of those legs tangling with hers, the thrust of that virile body moving over hers.

She loved him.

Was she going to lose him?

"I missed you, Twinkletoes," he said softly, a slow, sensual grin curving his well-formed lips.

"It's only been a few hours," she returned, crossing to the bed. She dropped her package and purse on the floor and sat down on the edge of the mattress.

"It feels longer. Much longer."

For neatness, she'd woven her hair into a long, loose French plait. Reaching up, he caught the thick, night-dark braid in one hand and gently pulled it, bringing her face down to his.

It was a teasing kiss. Her moist tongue flirted sweetly with his as she tasted the faintly minty flavor of his toothpaste. The clean scent of his warmth filled her nostrils.

"Mmm . . . nice," she murmured when they separated.

One golden-brown brow went up. "Just nice?"

"Very nice," she amended, turning her attention to the clutter on the bed. "What's all this?"

"Homework." Releasing her hair, he began gathering up the papers.

"For the game tomorrow? Do they computerize football?" While she knew statistics were playing an increasing role in television coverage of athletic events, she'd never dreamed there was this type of backgrounding.

"They computerize just about everything," he said wryly. "But no, actually, this is some information on a couple of investments I'm considering."

"Oh. How did things go at the stadium?"

"Just fine. Did you have a good day?"

"It was fun. I don't usually shop much in New York." She nodded toward the violet-sprigged box on the floor. "Would you like to see what I bought?"

His green-gold eyes glinted and she felt a delicious tremor of anticipation run up her spine. "Only if you promise to take it off if I don't like it."

"I promise," she replied sedately, then rose gracefully.

"Don't go away," she instructed him as she made her exit into the bathroom.

Shutting the door behind her, she shed her clothes quickly, uncharacteristically leaving the garments in a haphazard pile on the floor. Taking a deep breath, she opened the box that contained the negligee set and folded back the rustling layers of tissue paper.

It was a bewitching confection of nearly translucent silk and lace. The nightgown went on over her head, whisper-soft, the gossamer-fine fabric molding her delicate curves like a lover's caress. The short jacket that topped it was nothing but a drift of pale blush-pink with a threading of rose ribbon at the throat and cuffs.

As though fascinated by her own reflection, Melissa watched in the mirror as she carefully unbraided her hair and shook it loose. The glossy tumble waved down to the midpoint of her back. It was strange, she reflected suddenly, how much of her life she'd spent staring at her reflection, staring at the image of Melissa Stewart, dancer. At this moment she willed herself to see Melissa Stewart, woman.

She'd played temptresses before, donning the disguise of the sensual enchantress as she donned stage makeup and pointe shoes. A critic, seeing one such performance, had described her as "seduction incarnate."

But that had been onstage. Dancing. Now there was no music, no choreography. There was no audience. There was only her . . . and the man in the next room.

She heard the phone ring. Slowly she combed her fingers through her hair and then made a minuscule adjustment in the narrow ties that held the gown up.

Sean was on the phone, standing with his back to the bathroom on the far side of the bed, when she opened the door. She stood, poised for a moment, only half-registering what he was saying.

"I appreciate the invitation for dinner; I'll ask Melissa if she wants to . . ."

His voice trailed off as he turned and saw her. A blaze of desire, undisguised and unashamed, filled his eyes, and his nostrils flared. "My God—" he got out, his voice sounding as though it were stuck in the back of his throat.

"I think I'd like to eat in if you don't mind," she said huskily. The rhythmic rise and fall of her small breasts was hypnotically visible, and she could feel Sean's hot gaze marking it. Her nipples stiffened, erect and aching, against the sheer fabric of the gown.

"Look," he said in the receiver, his tone very much like the one he had used when he had instructed his chauffeur to drive them out to the airport and back. "I've just discovered we've got plans for tonight. I'll see you first thing tomorrow." He dropped the phone back into its cradle.

Melissa let a few heartbeats pass. "You once said you liked me in pink," she reminded him, flicking off the bathroom light and taking a few gliding steps into the bedroom.

He immediately picked up and placed the reference. "If I recall correctly, I also said I liked you *out* of pink."

With her natural dancer's grace, she covered the distance to the bed. They stood on opposite sides, separated only by the wide mattress. All they needed to do was to reach out to each other.

Melissa plucked at the delicate fabric of the negligee. "I promised I'd take it off if you didn't approve. What do you think?"

He gave a low, mocking chuckle, and she saw his large athletic hands clench briefly, as though he were exerting control over his body. She knew he was intrigued and aroused by her unexpectedly wanton behavior. She also sensed that he was willing to follow her lead . . . at least for the moment.

"Oh, I approve, my dark-haired darling. I also want you to take it off. Better yet, let me take it off."

She shook her head once, her ebony hair rippling with

the movement. "Not yet," she murmured, and moved slowly around the bed to confront him.

His eyes embraced her. His hungry stare reached into the secret places of her soul. Had she been unwilling, he could have seduced her with the heated jungle-cat caress of his gaze. But she was not unwilling.

The quicksilver sparkle in her eyes had melted to a sweet, beckoning softness. The curve of her lips—rosy like the ribbons of the negligee set—offered promises of passion. She undid the filmy pink jacket and slipped it off.

His hands went to the tie of his robe. She brushed his fingers away, a heart-jolting shock of electricity racing through her at the contact.

"No. I want to do it," she said. "Please."

A look of puzzlement flickered across his face, then disappeared, replaced by the unmistakable tension of growing sexual excitement. A low rumble issued from deep in his throat.

Melissa undid the belt with a gentle tug. Rising up on her toes, her dark head just coming level with his collarbone, she pressed a series of butterfly-light kisses across his broad chest. She nipped fleetingly at the tight circles of his nipples. The crispness of his chest hair tickled her soft lips. She blew at the tawny mat once or twice, feeling the ripple of reaction that ran through him with each puff of breath.

"Melissa—" He invoked her name in a way that was part pleading groan, part warning.

Emboldened by his response, Melissa ran her hands up his torso. Then very carefully she slipped off his robe. Taking a small step backward, she raised her hands to the slender knotted straps on her shoulders.

She danced her first real solo at age seventeen during the annual graduation performance for the MBT's school. She had always thought the excitement, the dizzying sense of triumph she had experienced that night, would remain unique in her life. She knew now she was wrong, gloriously wrong. Nothing could match the fiery fountain of love and wanting that was welling up inside her now. And nothing could equal the joy of sharing herself with this man . . . this perfect partner.

The nightgown slithered to the floor, falling around her feet in a pool of pink silk.

Sean sucked in his breath. "'The most exquisite thing I've ever seen . . .'" he quoted in a hushed voice. He celebrated the beauty of her nakedness with his eyes. With a feather-light touch he fingered the pink tips of her breasts, sending spirals of pleasure whizzing along her nerve endings. "And the most exquisite lover—"

He didn't finish the sentence. Melissa moved into his arms, fitting her supple delicate form against his hard virility. Her hands locked around his neck, pulling his head down. Who offered the first kiss, and who took it, was impossible to say.

They sank, side-by-side, onto the bed. Sean's fingers sought her with fevered but deliberate skill as her own hands traveled eagerly over his heated body, mapping its aroused masculine strength. Melissa shuddered as his tenderly expert ministrations brought her to the first plateau of pleasure.

"Sean—" she gasped out. "I want—"

"I know what you want, sweetheart," he returned hoarsely, his own breathing decidedly ragged.

But he didn't know. What she wanted was to tell him that she loved him, that she needed him. She wanted to tell him that tonight the pleasure was for him, that she was his.

But he was sweeping her to a place of throbbing, blinding sensations where words had no meaning. Touch, taste, sight, scent, and sound: she was dominated, overwhelmed by them. She was hurtling toward the center of her universe. It was an aching perfection of music and movement, but, at the elemental core, there was only Sean.

And when their passion soared to its final crescendo, exploding into rapture, Melissa clung to him, crying out her love.

Afterward, as she nestled against him, her eyes heavy, her lips swollen, and her brain drugged by the intensity of what she had experienced, Melissa thought she heard Sean whisper something into her hair.

But it was only a dream—she was already asleep. She had to be, because the words she thought she heard were the very ones she had wanted to say to him.

CHAPTER NINE

WHILE MELISSA HAD danced in several MBT productions that were broadcast on public television, she was unprepared for the amount of equipment and manpower required for a network sportscast. She was further amazed at how at ease Sean seemed in the midst of the electronic chaos. His popularity with the crew was clear from the unforced grins and friendly greetings he drew as he guided her, one arm possessively around her waist, through the setup.

"I wish you could stay up in the broadcast booth during the game," he said softly. "But the damn thing is a tight squeeze for the announcers."

"You don't think I could fit?" she asked with a little sigh, her wistful expression singularly at odds with the teasing edge she put on the question.

He laughed. "I think you could 'fit' just beautifully."

"Then?"

"Give me a break, you little witch! I'm going to have enough trouble concentrating on the game as it is."

"Why, Sean, do you find me a distraction?"

A technician passing by caught the question and the dazzling smile that accompanied it. The expression of frank admiration on his face indicated he'd answer the inquiry with an enthusiastic affirmative. A sharp, distinctly proprietary look from Sean drew a quick shrug of apology.

"I'm beginning to find you a public menace," Sean growled.

"And what's that supposed to mean?"

"Do you have any idea what you look like?"

Melissa glanced down at herself. Warned by Sean to dress for comfort, she'd donned a pair of denims, a white man-tailored shirt, and a mulberry and navy striped sweater. Her hair was neatly pulled back into a ponytail and she'd applied only a minimum of cosmetics—black mascara and a quick smudge of kohl pencil for her eyes, a sweep of blusher for her cheeks, and a smooth application of raspberry-tinted gloss for her lips.

"You don't like this outfit as well as the one I showed you last night, hmmm?"

"Melissa—"

"Of course, these are only plain old jeans. No designer labels—"

"Sweetheart, you do not need somebody's initials stitched on your—ah—"

"Mention the word *backfield* and you're in trouble."

"I was going to say *pockets*," he informed her dryly.

"Don't you like the way I look?"

"I'm crazy about the way you look. I just wish every male within eyeballing distance didn't feel the same way."

"Now you know how I felt at breakfast."

"Breakfast?" He gave her a puzzled glance. They'd

eaten downstairs at the hotel in the sprawling expanse known as the Lobby Court.

"Don't tell me you didn't notice the way that waitress was drooling over you. Actually her drool was landing on me, but it was directed at you."

"I must have missed her."

"And I suppose you missed the silicone starlet at the next table who was looking at you as though she'd like to spread you on toast?"

He simply grinned. "This is it," he said, directing her attention to a huge trailer. "Central command. Watch your step."

The thick gray cables running out of the trailer gave a hint of what it contained, but only a hint. With Sean at her back, Melissa found herself in a fully equipped, state-of-the-art television control room. Although it was still several hours before the start of the broadcast and the game, there was already an air of highly energized activity about the place.

One entire wall of the trailer was fitted with banks of monitors. A trio of good-sized color screens dominated the setup, but there were four long rows of small black and white televisions as well. Much of the floor space was crammed with video switching boards, audio control panels, and a full computer console. Melissa counted at least six reel-to-reel tape machines plus an equal number of cassette players.

A man Sean identified as Dan Forsythe, the director, was sitting in middle of everything, a headset slung around his neck, his eyes darting back and forth, and his hands gesturing explosively. He acknowledged their presence with a quick smile.

Fascinated, Melissa listened intently as Sean explained how the director could use the monitor bank to select from any one of dozens of shots from cameras located in the stadium or from the three cameras placed in the broadcast booth. She learned that the screen labeled LINE showed the picture he was feeding back to the network while the one directly to the left of it showed the shot he had readied to take next.

"I had no idea you used so many cameras for a single football game," Melissa marveled. "The ballet I did for PBS used only four."

Sean grinned. "In ballet the director knows where the dancers are going to be, thanks to the choreography. The coaches don't give out their game plans in advance in pro football."

"True."

"A lot of the cameras are used for 'iso' shots—that's for isolating particular elements of a play or for following one individual player."

"Mickey," Dan's voice commanded suddenly. "Mickey, if you can hear me on four, give me a signal."

Melissa's eyes swept the panel of monitors, locating the one marked with the number four. A second later the picture began moving up and down, as though the camera were nodding.

"Thank you, Mickey. Truck right a couple of feet, please. I want you to give me a lot of nice tight stuff to play with today. My on-air talent tells me this is going to be a very boring, one-sided game, so I'll need all the honey shots I can get."

"Honey shots'?" Melissa repeated, mystified.

"Shots of cheerleaders and pretty female fans," Sean explained with a glint in his eye.

"Man's favorite sport, hmmm?" she jibed.

Shortly afterward, Sean was called to the broadcast booth. He found Melissa a seat in the corner of the trailer and left her with a quick hard kiss.

The next few hours were fascinating, if rather confusing. Because of the monitor setup, Melissa was able to watch Sean the whole time, even when he wasn't actually on the air.

He looked devastatingly sexy and coolly comfortable under the camera's scrutiny. Unlike the other two announcers—both of whom seemed to require constant attention from a makeup artist and a hairdresser—Sean simply straightened his tie and, grinning, accepted a quick dusting of powder to take the glare off his forehead and nose.

Once the broadcast got under way, Melissa found herself deeply impressed by Sean's performance. Although he was the newest of the three announcers, he projected a charismatic mixture of knowledgeability and charm. He didn't talk as much as the other two, but when he spoke, his remarks were always informative and interesting. Drawing on his background as a player, he was able to predict likely strategies and to succinctly analyze what went right—or wrong—when those strategies unfolded.

He also had the electric knack of looking into the camera and communicating in a very direct and personal manner. Once or twice he flashed a quick smile at the lens, and while Melissa knew it was being seen by millions of viewers, she had the feeling it was meant especially for her. It was a smile that evoked her sweetest memories of their past together . . . and stirred her darkest anxieties about their future.

The flight back to New York after the game was an uneventful one. Melissa merely toyed with the elaborate first-class dinner offered by the beaming flight attendant and found herself drifting off to sleep when the movie— a complicated spy thriller—came on. She and Sean did little talking. He seemed curiously preoccupied, although he stroked her hair with tender fingers when she leaned her dark head drowsily against his shoulder at one point shortly before they landed.

There was a limousine waiting to pick them up at Kennedy Airport. At Melissa's request the car made a detour to Laurette Fishkin's Greenwich Village apartment so she could retrieve Nijinsky. The cat, she noticed with a trace of amusement, settled into the luxurious interior of the car with a rumbling purr that seemed to indicate he considered it no less than he deserved. He acknowledged Melissa's return by lapping casually at her fingers with his raspy tongue and then meowed a greeting in Sean's direction.

"Tomorrow, Twinkletoes?" Sean inquired softly when the car pulled up in front of her building. They'd agreed to spend the night apart.

Melissa nodded. "I'll cook dinner," she offered. "I—we should talk, Sean."

He was silent for a moment, his expression unreadable as his eyes searched her face. Melissa could feel her heart starting to thud painfully. She swallowed hard, hating the knot that was forming in her throat, threatening to choke her.

"Okay, Melissa. I'd like that."

With Nijinsky still curled comfortably on her lap, she leaned across the seat and kissed Sean. "Thank you for the weekend. I was so proud of you today. You were wonderful on the broadcast." She wanted to add that he was wonderful, period, but the words refused to come out. Something in his face—was it the quality of regret she thought she detected there?—kept her silent.

He returned the kiss but made no effort to deepen or prolong it. "Good night."

Plié!

First position, heels together, feet turned outward in a straight line. Head held proudly on a swanlike throat, the spine supple and erect, the body centered and in perfect balance.

Melissa's left hand rested lightly on the well-worn wooden bar. Her right arm, pale and slender, stretched out to the side. As she began the smooth descent into the grand plié, her arm moved downward, forward, then back to the side in a graceful flow. The curving line from shoulder to elbow to fingertip was flawless.

Reverse. Down, up. Slippers whispered softly across the floor as five dozen pairs of feet changed positions.

Relevé and hold . . . and hold.

Releasing the bar, Melissa arched her arms above her head as she rose up on pointe. She remained poised and motionless, her head tilted slightly as she studied her reflection out of the corner of her eye. With a ruthlessness she would never dream of turning on another person, she catalogued the minute signs of her six-and-a-half-week layoff.

She hadn't slept well the night before. Tossing and turning in her solitary bed, Melissa had rocketed between happiness and despair, confidence and sheer terror. Her dreams had been troubled and troubling. She'd seen herself standing in the wings of a great theater in Sean's arms, staring yearningly out at the stage while another ballerina danced to triumph in her role. She'd seen herself onstage, completely alone, bowing before an audience made up of endless rows of Verna Stewarts.

Would she sleep better tonight? Would she sleep alone?

A faint sheen of perspiration turned into rivulets of sweat. Normal breathing patterns were replaced by deep desperate gulps for energy-sustaining oxygen. A quiver of weariness blossomed into aching exhaustion and beyond.

But Melissa danced, just as she'd always danced.

"Welcome back," Laurette Fishkin grinned at the end of the class. "How are you holding up?"

Melissa toweled off her face and arms. "Aside from the fact that I think I died about thirty minutes ago, Laurette, I'm fine."

The other dancer nodded sympathetically. "It was that killer combination at the end that got to me." She grimaced, pulling a pack of cigarettes out of her tote bag.

"You know, I read in a magazine the other day that a lot of dancers are really masochists."

"You needed a magazine to tell you that?"

Laurette lit her cigarette, took a deep puff, then blew a smoke ring. "Well, it was nice to have a professional opinion on the matter. Hey, where'd you go over the weekend? Why were you so mysterious about it? You missed *The Red Shoes* at the Thalia," she added, referring to the famous 1948 ballet movie starring Moira Shearer as a doomed dancer. "I went—it was my fourth time. Wish you could've come. Or—maybe it's just as well? Maybe it would hit a little too close to home right now?"

Melissa knew what her friend was asking, but she wasn't ready to answer the question. She wasn't sure how to answer it. "I—I was out of town for the weekend," she said finally, untying her pointe shoes. "Sean was announcing a football game in Los Angeles and I went with him."

"Oh-ho!" There was a wealth of friendly innuendo in the two syllables.

"I was taking your advice about enjoying what I have while I have it."

"And?"

"And . . . I don't know yet. Sean—I—we're going to talk about things tonight." Her tone wavered between determination and apprehension.

"Look, it's going to be okay," Laurette assured her quickly. "So how long before you can start performing?"

"At least three weeks." Melissa was visibly relieved at the change of subject.

"At most, kiddo. I know you go into some kind of trance when you dance, so maybe you didn't notice, but the master of our fates, Bruno Franchiese, was prowling around during the last half of class. Those beady black eyes of his were glued to you most of the time."

"Mr. Franchiese's eyes aren't beady. Besides, he watches everybody."

"Not like he was watching you. I'll just bet he has special plans for you, Melissa."

The accuracy of Laurette's prediction was borne out about twenty minutes later when, after changing back into their street clothes, the two dancers paused to check the company bulletin board. About a dozen women from the corps were gathered in front of it, giggling and gossiping.

There were warm words of welcome and friendly cries of greeting as Melissa and Laurette approached. Melissa murmured a general hello. With characteristic thoughtfulness she paused to introduce herself to a dancer who'd joined the MBT company during her absence.

Laurette had neatly elbowed herself through the cluster of women and was scanning the schedule with a practiced eye. She stiffened suddenly, giving a low whistle. "Melissa," she drawled, "if you want to know why you-know-who was staring, take a look at this."

"This" made Melissa catch her breath when she read it. There, flamboyantly penned into the neatly typed roster of the company's daily activities, was the equivalent of an imperial summons: 3:00, STUDIO 2: M. STEWART AND Y. VOLNOY (NEW WORK - FRANCHIESE).

She was giddy with exhaustion by the time she finally left the theater late that afternoon. Although the session in Studio Two had been more discussion than dance, it had left her drained.

"A simple pas de deux," Franchiese had declared in deliberate understatement, explaining his concept with elegant theatrical gestures. But after hearing a tape of the throbbing rock-oriented music he had chosen, and after watching him mark out some of the steps he had created, Melissa knew it was going to be much more than that. Franchiese's intentions were complicated and contradictory and the flavor of the piece was unabashedly erotic.

Even in its nascent state it was clear the piece was going to be a triumph. For the second time in her career Melissa had been granted the ballerina's dream: to have a dance designed for *her*. If her mother were alive, she'd be crowing with exultation.

Yet Melissa felt as though she were being torn in half.

"You are thinking it is not like five years before when Franchiese makes *AfterImages* for you, *da?*" Yuri asked with unexpected perception as they left the rehearsal room after two grueling hours. Like her, he had grasped the promise and the implications of this new dance at the start.

Melissa nodded slowly, too bemused to do anything else.

"Maybe, *dushka*," the Russian declared carefully, "that is because *you* are not like before."

It was this thought that was whirling around inside her brain as she prepared dinner for Sean back at her apartment. She'd wanted to make something special for him, but the press of time and the rueful knowledge that her cooking skills were limited persuaded her that simplicity was the safest route. A hurried shopping expedition produced a menu of steak, baked potatoes, and salad.

It should have been easy to greet Sean at the door, to melt lovingly into his strong arms and turn her face up for his kiss, but it wasn't. After their passionate, unrestrained lovemaking of the weekend, there should have been no barriers between them, but there were.

"Melissa." His deep voice was velvet-soft and very steady as he stood, tall and dominantly masculine, in the foyer of her small apartment. His expression was carefully schooled and his cat eyes were guarded.

"Sean." She was pale and clearly uncertain. Her raven's-wing tumble of hair was clipped back off her face, revealing the classical purity of her features. While the swirling gray, violet, and deep rose tones of the caftan she was wearing underscored her air of ethereal fragility, the subtle cling of the fabric emphasized the supple perfection of her body.

"God, you are so beautiful," he said, sounding as though it hurt to make the admission.

"Thank you." She was trembling now. There was something desperately wrong. "I—there's some wine if you want it. Come in...please."

They maneuvered like attractive strangers for the next few minutes—careful, watchful, painfully polite. The laughing, demandingly tender man she had tumbled into love with had disappeared; in his place was an unquestionably sexy but disconcertingly distant individual she didn't know how to reach...and she was afraid to touch.

"I called you here at the apartment today," Sean said suddenly, draining his wine. Nijinsky was prowling around his feet. "Several times." He bent and scratched the animal's fluffy head. Melissa's body started to ache as she watched his long lean fingers move through the cat's fur.

"I—I was out all day. I had—I was very busy." *Tell him now,* a voice commanded. *Tell him everything.*

"Not so busy that you couldn't call Rita Perez."

She swallowed hard. It had been a difficult telephone call to make, but it had been something she'd had to do. As much as she'd come to love the work at the youth center—and as much as she hoped to find a way to continue doing it—she knew that getting back to top performance condition had to be her first priority. Rita had been understanding.

"You talked to Rita today?"

"She phoned me about some business."

"What did she say?" Melissa's fingers knotted together.

"She said you'd called to tell her that you weren't going to be able to help at the youth center any longer.

She said you'd told her you were sorry." His voice was very smooth until the last word. It was edged and sharpened with bitterness.

"I started taking class today," she said simply.

"You've been taking class for at least two weeks now."

"No. I mean *really* taking class." She lifted her chin, a mixture of entreaty and pride shining in her eyes. *Please, please, understand . . . my love,* she prayed silently.

"You've started dancing again." It was an accusation, quietly spoken, but an accusation nonetheless.

She nodded. "Mr. Franchiese wants . . . he—he's going to create a new ballet for me."

Sean started to laugh. It was a grating, humorless sound. "Congratulations, Melissa. You're getting what you want, aren't you? To say nothing of what your mother wanted." His sensual lips twisted into a mocking smile. "Well, bravo, babe."

"Sean—"

"Just tell me one thing," he interrupted. "I was under the impression you were supposed to stay out for another couple of weeks. What happened? Did your addiction to the drug you called dancing get too strong?"

She found herself on her feet. "I saw Dr. Goldberg. He said it was all right for me to start again."

He'd been toying with the stem of his wineglass as though he needed to occupy his hands in some harmless fashion. Now his fingers clenched around the fragile crystal. With an air of rigid control he set the glass down and stood up, too, facing her. "And just when did you go see Dave?"

"Friday." She moistened her lips, summoning up the courage to meet his gaze squarely. "Before we went to Los Angeles."

"Before we went . . ." He repeated the phrase musingly, his eyes jade-hard. There were only a few feet between them. He closed the distance in a single lithe

stride. Melissa had to fight down the urge to flinch or
to step back as he reached out and very gently traced the
curve of her cheek and jaw. "So, my dark-haired darling,
all the time we were together you knew, and you never
said a word. Tell me, how did you view this weekend?
As your—our—final engagement? Let me give you my
front-row review then: 'Miss Melissa Stewart gave one
hell of a farewell performance!'"

"Sean, no!" But even as she denied it she wondered
if there wasn't a kernel of truth in his accusation. She'd
known time was running out on them. Had her abandoned
behavior over the weekend in Los Angeles been the result
of a subconscious desire to prolong the pleasure . . . the
loving? "You can't think—"

"What have you been doing during the past six and
a half weeks?" he demanded savagely. "Checking the
days off on some secret calendar? Counting the hours
until you give yourself up again to the only thing you've
ever really cared about? Tell me, Melissa, was I anything
more than exercise for you? Did the great Franchiese
suggest that sex is a terrific form of physical therapy?"

She'd gone absolutely white. "How dare you!" she
exclaimed, her gray eyes glassy with rage. "I knew you'd
react this way."

"You knew nothing!"

"And you never understood the first thing about who
or what I am!" Verna Stewart had seen that, hadn't she?

His laughter was bitter. "What the hell is there to
understand beyond the fact that you're a dancer?"

"And what's wrong with that?"

"Not a damn thing," he answered acidly, his eyes hard
and his voice harsh. "But I happen to want a woman in
my life. That's what I need."

He'd said almost the same thing to her five years
before. It had hurt badly then. It hurt worse now. She'd
been a girl, an innocent girl, when she'd known him the

first time. Now she *was* a woman. And she'd allowed herself to believe deep in the secret places of her heart that she could be the woman for him.

"What you need ... what you want ..." she echoed. "What will you settle for?"

Sean sucked in his breath, his anger at the question an almost tangible thing. "Is that an offer? What are you willing to do? Schedule me in a couple of times a week like a masseur?"

She was being torn apart. *You're a dancer,* a little voiced jeered cruelly. *You're used to pain.*

"That day you took me to lunch after we met at the sports clinic you told me you were willing to settle for what you could get." If she'd cherished any illusions about the depth of his feelings for her, his last words had shattered them entirely. When he spoke of wanting and needing, he meant sex. She meant love.

Her mother had been right about that, too.

"And what I can get from you, apparently, is nothing!" For a brief unguarded moment the expression of his face altered to reveal a pain that seemed to match her own. "God, Melissa, after five years ... after what we've had during the past few weeks ... I was hoping that you'd finally realize—"

"Realize what? That I made a terrible mistake when I threw your ring and your proposal back in your face? Were you hoping that the past few weeks would persuade me that dancing isn't very important to me after all?"

"Melissa—"

"And all that sympathetic concern about my knee," she went on, not caring what she said. "Deep down you were probably hoping my injury would turn out to be something serious and permanent."

"Stop it!" Like a predator seizing its prey, he grabbed her upper arms and shook her once, very roughly. "Stop, damn it!"

Obedience—docility, even—was something valued

in a dancer. All her life Melissa had submitted to other people's directions—to her mother's, to her dance teachers', to Bruno Franchiese's . . . even to Sean's.

But now the prima ballerina was in full revolt and performing her own choreography. Melissa didn't even wince when Sean underscored his command by tightening his grip on her tender flesh.

"Why should I stop?" she flung at him coldly. "Have I hit a nerve, Sean? Just think, you could have gotten all your wants and needs taken care of if I'd had to stop dancing. It would have worked out just wonderfully for you! Too bad I wasn't crippled!"

He let go of her. The color had drained out of his face, leaving him pale beneath his tan. "You haven't just changed in five years, Melissa. You've become so twisted up, I hardly recognize you."

"Because I've learned to stand up for myself—because I really know what I want—I've become twisted?"

"What you want to do is dance." It was not a question.

"Yes." *I want to love you, too,* she added in her heart. *I want to do both!*

"Fine." His voice was devoid of inflection, his face empty of expression. The temper and the torment she had sensed in him only moments before were gone. Melissa felt achingly, agonizingly, alone.

It was almost a relief when he turned on his heel and walked away, letting himself out of the apartment without another word. She heard the lock click into place as he pulled the door shut behind him.

Five years ago she had run out of his apartment, slamming the door closed as hard as she could, trying to drown out the echoes of their painful parting. She had gone home to the satisfied gleam in her mother's eye and she had cried herself to sleep.

Melissa didn't cry this night. But she didn't sleep, either.

CHAPTER TEN

TWO WEEKS LATER Melissa sat on the floor of Studio Two, methodically massaging her right calf, patiently waiting for the muscle cramp that had seized her at the end of rehearsal to ease up. She flexed her foot experimentally, wincing at the twinge of pain that spiraled up her leg. It had been a long two hours with Bruno Franchiese and Yuri. While the new pas de deux was more than living up to the promise of its inception, it was still proving to be an incredibly demanding exercise. When Franchiese wasn't choreographing mind-boggling series of jumps and turns, he was commanding his dancers to perform excruciatingly drawn-out balancés.

Even the endlessly energetic Yuri had begun to look a bit drawn. He had also started muttering about Siberian labor camps.

But Melissa welcomed the work and the exhaustion. She wanted dancing to consume her again, to overwhelm

161

her life and to block out thoughts of everything else. She even welcomed the physical pain. It was, in its own minor way, a distraction from the emotional anguish that had been threatening to engulf her from the moment she heard the door click shut behind Sean.

There had been no word from him since that Monday night. Nor did she really expect there to be.

Maybe, she thought derisively, *we'll run into each other again in five years.*

In five years she would be over thirty. In the chronology of a dancer's life she'd be getting old. Other women would be moving into their prime. She'd be thinking about retiring.

You told me a dancer's life is short, Mama. You never told me what I'd do after mine was over. I'll have had the career you wanted, but where will I be? Alone, just as you said you were. I won't even have a daughter—

"Let me." It was Bruno Franchiese. He squatted down beside her on the floor and calmly moved her hands away from her leg.

Melissa started. She'd thought he'd left the room along with the rehearsal pianist and Yuri. "It's only a cramp," she said quickly.

He grunted wordlessly as he began kneading the muscle. He had broad-palmed spatulate-fingered hands, and there was a faint brown mottling on the back of them. His touch was sure and strong.

Sean's touch had been that . . . and so much more. She'd blossomed at the slightest brush of his long lean fingers. She'd flowered under the more intimate caresses. Her whole body ached with longing.

"Too tense," Franchiese declared disapprovingly, jerking her out of her train of thought. "You should relax . . . relax."

"It's—it's better now."

With a shake of his head he sat back on his heels and

studied her, a shrewd look in his dark eyes. While they weren't beady, as Laurette had suggested, they were disconcertingly direct.

"This ballet will be one of my best," he announced matter-of-factly. "We will use it for the end of the season gala and make the patrons happy."

"Like *AfterImages*." She hadn't really meant to say that and she certainly hadn't meant to sound so bitterly indifferent, but the parallels between now and five years ago were digging into her like crystalline shards of shattered glass.

"Yes . . . and no." He did not elaborate.

"It will be a beautiful ballet," Melissa said fiercely. It has to be. What else do I have left?

"It will be beautiful," he agreed. "And you will be miserable."

"No!" The protest was automatic but empty.

"Yes. My dear, I'm not blind. You are breaking your heart over someone, just as you did five years ago." His silver brows went up. "You seem surprised. Do you think all I notice when I watch my dancers is their bodies?"

Melissa sighed, her dove-colored eyes enormous in her delicate-featured face. She'd lost weight during the past two weeks. "No, of course not, Mr. Franchiese." She worried her lower lip for a moment, then gave him a crooked little smile. "I took your advice while I was out with my injury. I—I had an affair."

Franchiese took this admission in stride. "And you didn't get married."

She shook her head.

"But you did fall in love."

She gave a hollow laugh and brushed at a smudge of dust on her pale pink tights. "You didn't give me any advice about that."

"Love ruins some dancers," Franchiese said thoughtfully. "Others, it transforms."

Melissa stared at him questioningly for several sec
onds. "Did you ever meet a man named Sean Culhane?"
she asked suddenly.

"The athlete?" An odd smile tugged at a corner of the
older man's mouth. "A great cat of a man, as I recall."

"Then you do know him? I—he once said you'd talked
to him about me."

"Hmmm . . . we talked to each other about you. It was
a few days before you made your debut in *AfterImages*."

Melissa's eyes widened as she absorbed the impli
cations of this. Sean had spoken to Franchiese *after* they'd
broken up! But why?

"Did you—did you tell him you thought m-my sleep
ing with him had helped my dancing?" she blurted out,
ignoring the hot flush that mantled her cheeks as the
question came tumbling out.

"Very probably," came the imperturbable reply.

"What else did you say to him?"

"Not much. Simply that you were a very good dancer
who could become great, as you have."

The compliment left Melissa strangely unmoved. She
was too busy grappling with the other things Franchiese
had said.

"You are in love with this man?"

There was no need for her to speak.

Bruno Franchiese's hawkish features softened. "My
dear, consider one thing. Living—loving—is as much
of an art as the ballet. There are many times when we
dancers would do well to remember that fact."

"You look awful," Rita Perez told her bluntly, her
dark eyes flashing concern.

"Thanks, Rita, I needed that," Melissa responded flatly,
pulling off her slippers and tossing them unceremon
iously into her bag. By some fluke she'd discovered she
had nothing scheduled for this Thursday afternoon, so
she'd come up to the youth center. The children had

welcomed her with joyful enthusiasm. Rita had been more restrained.

"Have you seen yourself in a mirror recently?" They were sitting in the small cluttered room that served as Rita's office.

"I see myself in the mirror for several hours every day. It's part of what I do." She knew she was paler than usual and that she'd lost more weight than she could afford to. Laurette Fishkin had actually snatched a container of yogurt out of her hands the day before and dragged her off to a nearby sandwich shop. The redhead had then delivered a scathing lecture on nutrition and forced her to drink a huge chocolate milkshake.

"And do you like what you see?"

"Rita—"

"Actually I don't know which one of you looks worse. Sean's doing a pretty convincing imitation of death warmed over, too."

Just hearing his name hurt her. Melissa tried to hide her reaction by bending over and pulling her jeans out of her tote. She tugged them on over her thighs, not caring that the form-fitting denim was no longer form-fitting.

"I wouldn't know about that," she replied as evenly as she could, zipping up the front of the pants. "I haven't seen him in a while."

That wasn't completely true. The previous Sunday, sitting alone in her apartment, she had turned on the television and watched him. Her heart aching with the memories stirred by the mere sight of him, she had devoured him with her eyes. Time and again she'd reached out to change the channel, to end her self-inflicted torture, but she had been unable to do it.

Sean hadn't looked like death warmed over. The image on her small television screen had been vitally alive and devastatingly handsome. She'd seen no sign of strain, no indication of inner pain.

And no hint of love.

"Why haven't you seen him?" Rita demanded. "What's happened between the two of you?"

"Ask Sean."

"I have."

Melissa closed her eyes for a moment. She sank down into one of the rickety third-hand chairs that passed as furniture in the tiny office. "What did he say?"

"He told me to mind my own business."

Melissa opened her eyes and looked at the other woman. "Then why don't you?"

"Because two people I happen to care about are obviously in a great deal of pain!"

"Rita . . ." She was touched by the sincerity she heard. "Rita, there's nothing you can do. There's nothing anybody can do."

"Just tell me what happened."

"What happened is exactly what I knew was going to happen. I started dancing again and Sean couldn't accept it."

"Couldn't accept—what are you talking about? He's crazy about your dancing!"

Melissa gave a shaky laugh. "With *crazy* being the operative word. He resents the fact that I'm a dancer. If he had his way, I'd give up ballet and be—be—I don't know what I'd be."

Rita stared at her in disbelief. "Sean told you he wants you to stop dancing?"

"He didn't have to tell me. It was very clear." Sean wanted a woman in his life and he didn't think—he'd never thought—that she could be that woman and a ballerina, too.

There was a long silence.

"Melissa," Rita said slowly. "You know that Sean and I are good friends . . ."

"He told me you almost had an affair." It wasn't an accusation, simply a statement of fact.

"Ah—yes. Well, that was three or so years ago, right around the time Sean quit football. We dated. We were attracted to each other. And—and we probably would have become lovers if we hadn't gone to see you dance one night."

"Sean took you to see me?"

"Oh, he didn't say anything about you." The other woman grimaced slightly. "He didn't have to. The expression on his face when the curtain went up was enough. I knew there was no way he was ever going to look at me the way he was looking at the woman up there on the stage." She paused, allowing her words to sink in. "The woman was you."

"That was three years ago!"

"And in those three years he's seen you dance more times than I can count."

Melissa made a small choking sound and shook her head.

"Melissa," Rita persisted. "Melissa, he was in the audience for the matinee of *Giselle* when you got hurt. I was there with him. I thought you were terrific. The whole audience did—you got a half dozen curtain calls. But Sean knew there was something wrong when you started to dance Act Two. He was very worried."

"If he was so worried, why didn't he come back-stage?"

"How would you have reacted if he had?"

"I—" She tried to imagine the scene. She'd been close to fainting with pain after the performance. She'd been vulnerable and more than a little frightened. If Sean had suddenly materialized...

She might have turned on him like a wounded animal.

Or she might have flung herself into his arms.

"I don't know what I would have done, Rita," she said. "I don't know anything anymore."

*   *   *

Melissa Stewart stood in the wings of the New York State Theater . . . waiting. Her face was porcelain-pale, her gray eyes huge and unfocused. She moved through the stretches and bends of her warm-up with ritual precision and grace. The last reminder of her injury—an elasticized bandage—had been discarded in a heap along with her leg warmers.

In less than ten minutes she would be onstage, dancing before an audience for the first time in nearly three months. At the decree of Bruno Franchiese she would be performing *AfterImages* with Yuri Volnoy as her partner.

The evening was a virtual sellout. The crowd, to judge by its response to the program's first two presentations, was appreciative and knowledgeable. They would welcome her return, of course, but they would judge her as well.

Melissa had sent two tickets to Dr. Goldberg. A second pair had gone to Rita and Miguel Perez with an additional ticket for Tonio Martinez. The teenager—such a natural—had, in an unprecedentedly short amount of time, danced his way into a full scholarship at one of the most prestigious professional children's schools in the city.

She'd mailed one final ticket to Sean along with a note: *Please come. Love, Melissa.*

She'd hesitated a long time before writing the word *love*. It was not that she doubted her feelings. She simply feared his rejection of them.

Yet . . . he'd seen her dance! Not just once or twice, but over and over again.

Why?

He'd gone to Bruno Franchiese to discuss her career after they'd parted.

Why?

She'd been chasing the answers to these questions all week as she leapt and spun in class and rehearsals, but she'd never caught them. Perhaps she never would. Perhaps they weren't there to be caught.

She swept her leg up in the high kick of the grand jeté. To the front, side, back, side . . .

Would he be in the audience tonight?

Laurette materialized suddenly, a fuchsia flannel robe wrapped around her for warmth. She'd danced a solo in the first ballet of the program and was done for the evening. While she'd removed most of her stage cosmetics, she'd left her dramatically exotic eye makeup intact.

"I just looked into your dressing room, kiddo," she confided. "Everything but your couch is buried in blossoms. Usually you have to die to get that many flowers."

"Maybe my friends know something I don't," Melissa suggested wryly.

"Ha-ha," the redhead retorted with a friendly grimace. "You're going to be terrific and you know it. My God, the orchestra actually applauded you yesterday during rehearsal! The last time they clapped for anybody was when what's-her-name, the Swedish meatball, lost her top during that awful Stravinsky variation two seasons ago."

"I don't think they'd notice if I lost my top," Melissa murmured, pausing in her warm-up while she made a small adjustment in the hang of her costume. The simple garment was a one-shouldered draped affair that barely brushed the tops of her slender thighs. The fabric was pristine white shot with fine silver and gold metallic threads.

It was an enchantingly ethereal outfit. It also ruthlessly revealed the dwindling fragility of her figure.

"Don't even think about something like that!" Laurette commanded superstitiously. "It's bad luck."

"I didn't get any pink roses," Melissa said suddenly, her softly rouged lips curving downward with a trace of wistfulness.

"What?" Melissa's hair was done up in the requisite

ballerina's bun. Laurette, frowning critically, reached over and pushed a slightly protruding bobby pin back into its proper place.

"My lucky flowers, remember? Pink tea roses and baby's breath."

"Oh—you mean the ones from your nameless admirer?"

Melissa nodded her dark head slowly. She had already seen the flower arrangements of every imaginable size and shape that Laurette had referred to. Crowded into her tiny dressing room, they transformed the drab, utilitarian cubicle into a sweetly perfumed bower. She'd been flattered by the unexpected outpouring from her admirers and was deeply touched by the little bouquet sent from her class at the youth center. But she'd felt a curious pang of disappointment when she'd realized, after careful inventory, that there were no anonymous pink tea roses.

"My admirer is probably somebody else's by now," she said quietly.

"I doubt that." With an understanding smile Laurette kissed her fingertips and pressed them lightly to Melissa's cheek, taking care not to smudge the blush applied there. She whispered the French vulgarity that dancers invoke in the name of luck. Melissa smiled her thanks.

Then it was time to dance.

AfterImages began with an intricate pas de quatre with three other female dancers. Although the quartet of ballerinas began as equals, subtle shifts in positioning and variations in the choreography spotlighted Melissa. Inevitably, irresistibly, she emerged from the group, her quicksilver body spinning in double and triple fouettés where the others performed only singles. The aching clarity of her balancés remained frozen in jewellike perfection. Gradually the others vanished, leaving Melissa to be seduced into a fiery pas de deux with Yuri.

He'd said they had something special onstage, and

they did. Yet, even as he molded her against him, even as he lifted her in soaring triumph, Melissa knew she was only echoing, only palely evoking, the passion she had experienced with Sean.

The pas de deux ended with a sudden blackout and silence. Melissa was only dimly aware of the thunder of applause that rolled up out of the audience, only fleetingly conscious of the way Yuri found her hand in the darkness and pressed a quick kiss to it before scampering off into the wings.

When the spotlight hit her, igniting yet another explosion of applause, she was alone.

Music and movement. The first season she had danced the solo in *AfterImages* she had been consumed by it. It had been her escape from the memories, from the yearnings, that crowded in on her whenever she thought of how she had lost Sean.

As the pain of that loss had eased, her interpretation of the solo had changed. Artistry replaced anguish, and discipline took the place of desperation.

Tonight with shattering beauty she poured her very soul into the dance. Her soul, but not her heart. Her heart was already pledged. If, once or twice, her body rather than Bruno Franchiese dictated the steps, no one noticed. She danced for her life, for her love, for herself.

All the while she kept hoping that Sean was in the audience, watching, and that he understood she was dancing for him as well.

She lost count of the number of curtain calls afterward. Like an exquisitely drilled puppet, she made her reverences, acknowledging the bravas and the cheers. Receiving a staggering sheaf of flowers from a tuxedoed gentleman she only slightly recognized, she automatically plucked out a blossom and offered it to Yuri. Hand on his heart in a gesture of faultless gallantry, he executed a bow and accepted it.

The madness and excitement out front infected everybody backstage. Melissa was kissed and congratulated by everyone from a burly stagehand to Bruno Franchiese himself as she made her way back to her dressing room.

The fans descended and she was gracious. Her friends—Rita, Miguel, and Tonio—showed up as well, and she was grateful.

Sean did not come.

Alone at last and conscious of a bone-deep exhaustion, Melissa undid her pointe shoes. The fragile construct of canvas, glue, thread, and satin had served well. Another wearing—perhaps two in class—and the slippers would be discarded.

She stripped off her costume and peeled out of her flesh-toned tights. Shivering a little, she wrapped herself in a robe before sitting down at her dressing table. Hunting through the masses of flowers, she located a huge, partially used jar of cold cream. Carefully she cleansed the coating of cosmetics from her face. She tossed a handful of crumpled, soiled tissues into an overflowing wastebasket next to the dressing table.

As a principal dancer, Melissa had a private shower as well as a private dressing room. She took full advantage of the situation now, luxuriating under the hot spray for at least ten minutes, sighing with pleasure as the post-performance tension began to seep out of her body. It was a pity there was nothing as simple to do to ease the emptiness within her heart.

She was out of the shower, wrapped in the robe once again and vigorously brushing out her dark hair when there was a knock at the door.

"Just a minute," she called, pausing to retrieve a scattering of hairpins from the floor. Rising gracefully, she flipped the night-dark tumble of her hair back off her shoulders and crossed to the door. "I'm sorry to keep you waiting," she apologized as she opened it with a soft smile. "But I was—oh!"

The exclamation was barely audible. It was more an intake of breath than anything else.

Sean stood in the doorway. There was a wary uncertainty in the depths of his green-gold eyes and a definite edginess in his stance. His lean features were carefully schooled. There was a hint of strain in the set of his firm jaw.

She made a distracted gesture. He apparently took it as an invitation because the next thing she knew, he had stepped into the tiny dressing room. He shut the door with a smooth, deliberate movement. She heard the lock click into place.

He looked so devastatingly strong, so utterly male, standing there in the midst of the feminine theatrical clutter. Only a few feet separated them. Melissa wanted to reach out and touch him, to reassure herself that he was as warmly real as he seemed. She wanted to press herself against his broad, unyielding chest and hear the steady beating of his heart beneath the beautifully tailored midnight-blue suit and white silk shirt.

Then she saw the flowers. What little color she had drained out of her cheeks.

"I thought it was time your anonymous admirer made himself known," Sean said quietly, holding out an exquisite bouquet of pink tea roses and baby's breath.

Her hands were trembling so hard, she nearly dropped the bouquet as she took it from him. Their fingers brushed for an electric instant, touching off a starshower of reaction that rippled through her body in a dizzying rush.

"All this time?" she asked shakily.

"All this time," he confirmed.

Once before that evening she had given herself up to a man's embrace. She had feigned the melting surrender called for by the *AfterImages* choreographer, with professional expertise. She had been in total command during an act that was supposed to represent complete abandon.

There was nothing controlled, nothing remotely
professional, about the way she offered herself to Sean
now. Rather than melting, she caught fire. She took as
well as she gave, eagerly straining against his hardness,
willingly parting her lips to receive the triumphant probe
of his moist tongue, then countering with a sweetly provocative thrust of her own.

The bouquet tumbled to the floor as her arms swept
up, circling his neck. Her fingers tangled in the crisp
tawniness of his hair. She arched sinuously, glorying in
the shudder of response she felt well up through his lean
body.

His mouth slipped down the fine line of her throat.
She felt his fingers tug impatiently at the collar of her
robe. He nuzzled hungrily at the satiny joining of her
shoulder and neck, nipping at her bare quivering flesh
as though it were an exotic delicacy.

"God, you're so beautiful. But so fragile," he murmured heatedly, his palms sliding possessively down her
back and cradling her slender hips. "Skin like silk, bones
like crystal—"

"I won't break, Sean," she assured him fiercely. "Love
me, please, love me!"

Groaning, he sought her mouth again. "I do, love,"
he said against the softness of her lips. The kiss they
shared was lingering and honeyed. "Love me back,
sweetheart," he encouraged huskily. "Love me and be
my wife."

Her heart missed a beat. "Your w-wife?" she whispered. "You want me to marry you?"

"Now more than ever."

"What about my-my dancing?"

She felt him stiffen and experienced a terrible stab of
fear. If it was coming to a choice again—

"I'll give it up!" she blurted out.

"No!" The word came out of him explosively. He
pulled back from her, his jungle-cat eyes molten. "No,

damn it, you will not give it up. I want a whole woman for my wife, Melissa. I love all of you, don't you understand? And that includes the very beautiful, very special part of you that dances."

"But five years ago—"

"Five years ago neither one of us was ready for what we were reaching for. I was caught up in being Mr. Super Jock and you were . . . you were the budding ballerina. You were so inexperienced and innocent. I was just plain insensitive." The anger in his eyes cooled slightly.

Insensitive? This from a man who had tenderly gentled her fears about becoming a woman? Who had initiated her into the realities of ecstatic, generous passion?

"Oh, sweetheart, it was easy to be sensitive when I was making love with you," he said softly, stroking her cheek. "Melissa, if anybody had asked me five years ago what I felt about your dancing, I would have told them I thought it was terrific. On a conscious level I was proud of your talent and what you were doing with it. But underneath I resented it. All those things you accused me of . . . I was jealous as hell, babe."

"Jealous?"

He gave a humorless laugh. "Yeah, jealous. You'd already given sixteen years of your life to the ballet when I met you! How could I compete with that? Dancing took you places I couldn't reach. It gave you things—seemed to fill you up—"

Her gray eyes went cloudy. "Oh, Sean—" she breathed, wondering at her blindness . . . and his. All this time she'd thought he didn't understand what dancing meant to her. In reality he understood far too well. What he didn't see, what she hadn't been able to show him, was that he had come to mean so much more.

"I never would have asked you to quit," he went on painfully, his expression bitterly reflective. "But I would have found some way to . . . Melissa, you were so damned malleable five years ago. You bent the way people told you to. Hell, that's how you'd been trained! If we'd stayed together back then, I think you would have backed off your dancing dreams to please me. And that would have ruined us sooner or later."

Melissa swallowed convulsively. Her palms were moist and her heart was pounding. "And now?"

"And now. . . . I went to see Franchiese after we broke up, you know. I don't know why exactly. It wasn't a very rational period in my life. He didn't say much at first, just looked me up and down very appraisingly and muttered something about being glad to meet the man who'd done so much for your dancing!" There was a mocking flash of dimple at this last comment. "We talked. What it came down to was him telling me to leave you so you could grow up—as a dancer and as a woman. And that, my love, is what you've done."

A shimmer of tears lent a silvery sheen to Melissa's eyes. She blinked them away, feeling herself start to flower in the warmth and tenderness of Sean's expression.

"But why did you wait five years?"

He sighed. "There were so many reasons. Some good, some lousy. I nursed a lot of hurt and anger over you, Melissa. And I won't lie. I did my best to forget you. I had my work and I had a lot of other women. Then one night I took a lady I thought I might be able to get serious about to the ballet."

"Rita Perez."

His sensual lips twisted into a rueful, crooked smile. "Yeah, Rita. It was supposed to be a test. I wanted to prove I could see you again and not feel anything. God! The curtain went up and all I did was feel! It was a—a revelation. Before, when I'd seen you dance, it was always a very proprietary thing. You were *my* girlfriend up there onstage. But that night it was all you. You were your own woman. The next day I bought tickets for every damned performance you were scheduled to dance. I also put in a standing order with a florist."

Melissa bent her head, pressing her brow against his chest. "I thought about you so many times," she whispered. "I wanted you so badly...loved you so much. I tried to lose myself, to bury those feelings in my dancing. For a time I think it worked. At least I was numb. But now—" She looked up at him, her face very vulnerable. "That day in the sports medicine clinic I knew I could dance myself to death and never get over you."

Sean expelled a breath. He touched her cheek with unsteady fingers. "My being there that day wasn't a matter of chance," he confessed.

"What?"

"Oh, hell, Melissa, I'd waited and watched so long—I was in the audience that night, and I knew you were hurt. I figured if you were hurt badly enough, you might go to a doctor. I knew you trusted the clinic from before, so I crossed my fingers and called them. To make a long story short, the receptionist is a sucker for romance. I wheedled your appointment time out of her. Then I made my own appointment."

Her mouth dropped open. "But you said you'd run into a wall!"

"I did...about a year ago. I made up some story about my shoulder acting up again."

"Sean!"

"What I should have told them is that five years ago I fell like a ton of bricks for a beautiful ballerina."

She gave a breathless little laugh. "I love you, Sean Culhane."

He framed her face with gentle palms. "A few minutes ago you seemed to say you loved me enough to give up your dancing. Do you love me enough to keep dancing and marry me?"

Her heart was full of happiness. "Oh, yes!"

"It won't always be easy, but we can work it out,"

he promised. "Your schedule . . . my schedule, but we'll find the time we need."

Melissa nodded, sharing his confidence. It would take effort and energy . . . and compromise. But it was what they both wanted. "We'll make the most of the time we find," she pledged in turn. "And when we're apart—"

"We can think about how terrific it'll be when we get back together," he completed huskily. He began to stroke her with slow, sensuous deliberation, easing his hands over her body, telling her by his touch that he was as aware of the nakedness beneath the robe as she was.

She molded herself against him with a sigh, her fingers seeking the knot of his tie. She tugged at it blindly, then began undoing the buttons of his shirt. She was lost in a glowing, pulsing web of sensation.

But not so lost that she didn't realize what Sean was murmuring into her hair.

"If you have any doubts, ever, tell me. We're both strong enough to be honest with each other this time. That was the worst of it five years ago. If you'd been able to explain what you were feeling instead of sending your mother—Melissa?"

He must have felt the sudden rigidity in her body. Melissa pulled away from him, not caring that her robe was gaping open to the waist. "My mother?" she repeated in a choked voice.

"I understand why you did it," he said urgently. "God knows, I didn't then, but I think I do now. Finding out about your father, whoever he was, and about how much your mother felt she gave up to have you, it's no wonder you were torn up. But hearing it from somebody else, it hurt, Melissa. To have to sit there and listen to another person telling me what was going on inside your head—"

"What are you talking about?" she asked in desperate bewilderment.

"I'm talking about your mother coming to see me after we got engaged. She told me you weren't sure—"

"What?"

"She said you'd asked her—" His eyes narrowed. "You didn't know anything about it, did you?" he asked in a taut voice.

Melissa shook her head.

He cursed under his breath. "What about our fight? You did want to postpone the wedding until after you made your debut in *AfterImages*."

"I didn't! I mean, I was so confused. Mama kept harping on what had happened to her. She kept telling me I couldn't be a dancer and a wife. She kept—oh, Sean!" She saw the truth suddenly, and it made her sick.

He gathered her up against him, his embrace fiercely protective. "It doesn't matter," he said harshly.

"But it does." She was trembling with hurt and impotent fury. She hadn't just been malleable. She'd been manipulated over and over again, and she'd never realized what was going on. "We lost five years!"

"It doesn't matter," he repeated. "Not now. What's five years compared with the rest of our lives?"

She went very still. The passionate promise in his simple words broke over her like a crystalline wave, washing away her bitterness at her mother, cleansing her of all doubts.

No, it wouldn't always be easy for them, but it would be worth it.

A dancer's life is very short. That was a fact.

So what? Melissa thought with a sudden spurt of triumph. *I'm much more than a dancer!*

"When does it begin?" she asked hoarsely, turning her face up in conscious invitation.

"What?"

"The rest of our lives together."

"Right now."

"Here?"

"With all these flowers?"

"You can pretend you died and went to heaven."

"With you, Twinkletoes, I don't have to pretend went to heaven." His hands closed over her bare breasts coaxing the delicate mounds to aching arousal. His thumb teased the rosy peaks with feathery caresses, making them stiffen with the yearning evidence of her receptiv ity.

She pulled his shirt free of his belt with an impatien gesture, eager to feel the tempered strength of his nake body against hers. Her hands danced erotically over hi chest.

He kissed her deeply, demandingly, drinking in the flavor of her. "You didn't have anything on underneath that white incitement to seduction tonight, did you?" h asked.

"Just my tights." She smiled.

"I had to sit there, squirming, with the program sprea over my lap the whole time," he whispered in her ear licking the lobe teasingly before kissing a path back t her mouth.

Melissa was doing a fair amount of squirming hersel at that point. "Just remember, Mr. Franchiese didn't de cide to make *AfterImages* for me until after I went to be with you. And—oh, please! H-he didn't start this ne ballet until we were—ah, Sean!"

"At the rate we're going, my love, the next ballet h choreographs for you is going to be X rated." He scoope her up in his arms. "Are you sure you want to do thi here? I have a limo outside—"

"Here first, then . . . the . . . limo." She pressed arden little kisses along the curve of his jaw, nibbling at hi flesh as she went along.

He crossed to the couch in the corner of the room i two long strides, not caring that he knocked over thre floral arrangements as he did so. "You think we'll deserve an encore?" he teased, laying her down against the cushions. He began shedding his clothes with neat, economical movements.

The expression that bloomed across Melissa's face, bringing a luminous softness to her dove-gray eyes and a tantalizing curve to her lips, was not her practiced dancer's smile. It was the smile of a woman who loves — and knows herself to be loved in return.

She raised her arms out to him. "We'll deserve an encore," she assured him.

WONDERFUL ROMANCE NEWS!

Do you know about the exciting SECOND CHANCE AT LOVE/TO HAVE AND TO HOLD newsletter? Are you on our *free* mailing list? If reading all about your favorite authors, getting sneak previews of their latest releases, and being filled in on all the latest happenings and events in the romance world sounds good to you, then you'll love our SECOND CHANCE AT LOVE and TO HAVE AND TO HOLD Romance News.

If you'd like to be added to our mailing list, just fill out the coupon below and send it in…and we'll send you your *free* newsletter every three months — hot off the press.

□ *Yes, I would like to receive your free SECOND CHANCE AT LOVE/TO HAVE AND TO HOLD newsletter.*

Name _____

Address _____

City _____ **State/Zip** _____

Please return this coupon to:

    Berkley Publishing
    200 Madison Avenue, New York, New York 10016
    Att: Rebecca Kaufman

HERE'S WHAT READERS ARE SAYING ABOUT

Second Chance at Love®

™

"I think your books are great. I love to read them, as does my family."
— *P. C., Milford, MA**

"Your books are some of the best romances I've read."
— *M. B., Zeeland, MI**

"SECOND CHANCE AT LOVE is my favorite line of romance novels."
— *L. B., Springfield, VA**

"I think SECOND CHANCE AT LOVE books are terrific. I married my 'Second Chance' over 15 years ago. I truly believe love is lovelier the second time around!"
— *P. P., Houston, TX**

"I enjoy your books tremendously."
— *I. S., Bayonne, NJ**

"I love your books and read them all the time. Keep them coming—they're just great."
— *G. L., Brookfield, CT**

"SECOND CHANCE AT LOVE books are definitely the best.!"
— *D. P., Wabash, IN**

*Name and address available upon request

Second Chance at Love.

___07803-4	SURPRISED BY LOVE #187	Jasmine Craig
___07804-2	FLIGHTS OF FANCY #188	Linda Barlow
___07805-0	STARFIRE #189	Lee Williams
___07806-9	MOONLIGHT RHAPSODY #190	Kay Robbins
___07807-7	SPELLBOUND #191	Kate Nevins
___07808-5	LOVE THY NEIGHBOR #192	Frances Davies
___07809-3	LADY WITH A PAST #193	Elissa Curry
___07810-7	TOUCHED BY LIGHTNING #194	Helen Carter
___07811-5	NIGHT FLAME #195	Sarah Crewe
___07812-3	SOMETIMES A LADY #196	Jocelyn Day
___07813-1	COUNTRY PLEASURES #197	Lauren Fox
___07814-X	TOO CLOSE FOR COMFORT #198	Liz Grady
___07815-8	KISSES INCOGNITO #199	Christa Merlin
___07816-6	HEAD OVER HEELS #200	Nicola Andrews
___07817-4	BRIEF ENCHANTMENT #201	Susanna Collins
___07818-2	INTO THE WHIRLWIND #202	Laurel Blake
___07819-0	HEAVEN ON EARTH #203	Mary Haskell
___07820-4	BELOVED ADVERSARY #204	Thea Frederick
___07821-2	SEASWEPT #205	Maureen Norris
___07822-0	WANTON WAYS #206	Katherine Granger
___07823-9	A TEMPTING MAGIC #207	Judith Yates
___07956-1	HEART IN HIDING #208	Francine Rivers
___07957-X	DREAMS OF GOLD AND AMBER #209	Robin Lynn
___07958-8	TOUCH OF MOONLIGHT #210	Liz Grady
___07959-6	ONE MORE TOMORROW #211	Aimée Duvall
___07960-X	SILKEN LONGINGS #212	Sharon Francis
___07961-8	BLACK LACE AND PEARLS #213	Elissa Curry
___08070-5	SWEET SPLENDOR #214	Diana Mars
___08071-3	BREAKFAST WITH TIFFANY #215	Kate Nevins
___08072-1	PILLOW TALK #216	Lee Williams
___08073-X	WINNING WAYS #217	Christina Dair
___08074-8	RULES OF THE GAME #218	Nicola Andrews
___08075-6	ENCORE #219	Carole Buck

All of the above titles are $1.95
Prices may be slightly higher in Canada.

Available at your local bookstore or return this form to:

SECOND CHANCE AT LOVE
Book Mailing Service
P.O. Box 690, Rockville Centre, NY 11571

Please send me the titles checked above. I enclose _____ Include 75¢ for postage and handling if one book is ordered; 25¢ per book for two or more not to exceed $1.75. California, Illinois, New York and Tennessee residents please add sales tax.

NAME _____

ADDRESS _____

CITY _____ STATE/ZIP _____

(allow six weeks for delivery)   SK-41b